MANIFEST

Printed in Australia
First Printing: October 2022
Shawline Publishing Group Pty Ltd
www.shawlinepublishing.com.au

Paperback ISBN 978-1-9228-5053-9
eBook ISBN 978-1-9228-5060-7

 A catalogue record for this
work is available from the
National Library of Australia

OLIVIA HILLIER

This is for all the girls who grew up believing
Sleeping Beauty only woke up after a kiss from a man.
Queen please, the crown is already yours.

Chapter 1

'Hello darling, what's your name?' A lady with long, curly brown hair smiled at me from behind the white-clothed table covered in name badges.

'Daphne Holmes,' I said, standing up straight and smiling back at her.

I was excited for the day—well, no, I wasn't excited for the day. I was excited for the day to be over so I could get home and tell Levi how he had changed my life.

The woman stood up from behind the table and spoke again. 'Welcome, Daphne.' She wore a cream ribbed dress that looked like it had been tailor-made for her. She scanned the table of alphabetically arranged name tags and handed me one. 'We're so glad you're here. Casey is going to be the facilitator of our program today. She's great—one of our best. She's flown here all the way from Los Angeles.' The woman spoke with great enthusiasm. 'Have you got a pen and paper with you? You're going to want to write a lot down.'

I grabbed my small pink journal and gold pen out of my handbag. 'All good to go.' I smiled back wide-eyed at the woman. 'Is there anything else I need?' I wasn't quite sure what I was doing here, but Levi said it would be a good idea and that was more than enough reason to spend two nights out of town.

'All you need is yourself, darling.' The woman grinned. 'The seminar should start in approximately fifteen minutes.' She pointed at two large doors to the left of her where many people were entering one by one. 'You can enter the auditorium quietly through these doors. Find yourself a seat and get familiar with the space. Now, it's a big day. We fit a whole lot in for your benefit. Anytime you need something to eat or drink, just quietly make your way to the back of the room and our lovely volunteers will serve you. Other than that, have fun.'

I smiled. 'Thanks, I can't wait!'

I stood at the back of the room, scanning the crowd. I couldn't believe how many people were in attendance. The auditorium looked as though it seated thousands. There was another level of seating above me; I could see silhouettes of people under the bright lights, scattered amongst the tall ceiling. Everyone sat quietly, staring blankly at the empty stage. I found a seat that appeared to be free in the middle of the room, just a couple of seats in from the walkway. I quickly sat down.

I'd never been in a room with so many people that was engulfed in such an eerie silence. One wrong move would echo throughout the whole room.

'I like your skirt,' the girl sitting beside me whispered in my ear. I smiled back at her. She looked close to my age—twenty-two. She wore bright orange lipstick and a silver headband shined in her long flaming hair that almost matched the colour of her lips.

She was talking about my knee-length peach skirt and how it looked so cute with my white bodysuit. 'Thanks,' I replied. I must have spoken a little too loud. I watched as heads turned back towards me. I leaned in closer and whispered back to the girl, 'I bought it yesterday from this really cute boutique not too far from here. It was only twenty dollars.'

'Bargain,' she whispered, smiling.

Music started blaring across the auditorium. The blue stage lights circled the crowd and then snapped back to the stage, where a tall, lean woman appeared with a bright smile that rivalled the woman who welcomed me in. She had the straightest platinum blonde hair I'd ever seen, cut into a long blunt bob. She wore a white bodysuit not too different from the one I was wearing, but she'd paired it with some black work pants and a pair of pointy heels. The silent room burst out into a roar of applause. Groups of people jumped up out of their seats, clapping and dancing. I sat frozen, unsure of what I'd walked into. I felt like I was on an episode of *Ellen*. The gorgeous woman on stage started to make her way down through the aisles of seats and dancing patrons.

The girl sitting next to me leaned in a little too close, her lips only a centre metre away from my ear, this time speaking loudly over the music and cheering. 'So, what did you come here for?'

'I don't even really know what this is?' I shouted back, confused.

'What do you mean?' She broke into laughter. 'How did you find out about Tuned In?'

'My boyfriend.' I paused and quickly corrected myself. 'Well, he's not my boyfriend. This guy I have been seeing back home told me about it. He thought it would be a good idea for me to come along. I think it's like the last thing he wants from me—to take interest in something that means a lot to him. After this seminar I think he is going to make our relationship official.'

Her lips drooped and her eyes squinted slightly. 'Well, this will probably be a little bit of an awakening for you. Have you watched any of Tuned In's content before?'

I shook my head. 'Why are you here?'

'I'm working on really scaling my business,' she replied.

The music in the room started to lower and the crowd of people sat back down in their seats. The blonde woman returned to the stage.

'Hello everyone!' she said loudly into the microphone she wore around her face. The crowd applauded her welcome. 'Welcome to Tuned In or TI as you'll hear me call it throughout this magnificent manifesting day we get to spend together! My name is Casey,' she said even louder in her strong American accent and the crowd roared again. 'Now, can I please have a show of hands for those that are returning members to our seminar?'

I looked around the room, about a third of people had thrown their hands up in the air. 'We are so glad to have you back. Today is going to be a whole new journey that will help you build upon everything you have learnt from previous seminars. And that must mean the rest of you are TI virgins. I am so glad that I get to be the presenter that pops your Tuned In cherry today!' The room laughed. 'In all seriousness though, if this is your first seminar, I am thrilled that you're all here because today is about to be the first day of a whole new life for you. The life that you have dreamed of. The life that you've held at an arms-reach for too many years because of excuses, stories, fears and worries. This is what holds you back from stepping into the life that you were destined to lead. Are you ready to step into your full potential?'

The crowd screamed out a large *yes* in unison.

'Are you ready to really see what you're made of?'

'YES!' the crowd screamed out again.

'Are you ready to let go of everything that has been holding you back and get everything you've ever dreamed of?'

'YES!' This time I joined in with the enthusiasm of the crowd. The energy of the room gave me goosebumps.

'Okay, let's get going!' A man dressed in black walked swiftly onto the stage and placed a stool and a bottle of water in the very middle. Casey took a seat and the two large screens behind her switched on with a close-up of her face.

'Just some bookkeeping before we get started. This is going to be a long day. I would really appreciate it if everyone could have their mobile phones switched off and keep a pen and paper handy to take notes. If you need to eat, please quietly make your way towards the back of the room where we have our lovely volunteers serving up snacks and drinks all day to get us through. Bathrooms can also be found at the back of the room through the far-left door. If you have any other questions throughout the day, please go and see our volunteers at the back of the room.' Casey paused and reached down to take a sip from the water bottle beside her stool. 'Now we can begin,' she continued. Her eyes gleamed and her smile grew bigger as she scanned the room. 'I want to begin by asking you all two questions: why did you come here today? What knowledge do you want to walk away with after today? I want you all to take a moment to write it down for me.'

The stage lights dimmed while the lights in the audience brightened. Everybody reached for a pen and paper. I pulled my pink notebook and favourite gold pen out of my bag. I crossed my left leg over my right, balanced my notebook and started writing.

I came today to make Levi commit to me.

It was simple—to the point. Seeing the words written out neatly in my cursive scrawl heightened my excitement. I felt my heart do a small flip as I closed my notebook and stared back up at the stage. People were still writing.

Casey's voice boomed out to the crowd. 'Whatever you're writing into existence right now, whatever intention you are setting in stone with your pen in hand, I want you to know you are in the right place to make these dreams a reality.'

I smiled at Casey. I felt as though she was speaking right at me. I still wasn't sure how Tuned In would bring my dreams to fruition, but so far, I was glad I'd made it here.

'Okay, enough writing.' Casey stood up and walked towards the end of the stage. 'I want to start hearing from you. I need to know all the dreams that we are going to start creating here today.'

As Casey stood at the edge of the stage, volunteers dressed in black dispersed into the audience, each holding a microphone. Casey pointed to a seat in the front row. A volunteer promptly darted over. 'You, lovely lady, tell me your name and why you came here today.'

The screens behind Casey changed from a close-up of her to a close-up of a middle-aged woman with a brunette bob. She took the microphone from the volunteer.

'I'm Jeanette.' Her smile lit up the screens. 'This is my first time at Tuned In and I'm really excited to be here.' Her voice was both nervous and excited as it echoed through the auditorium. 'I'm here with my daughter, she was the one who introduced me to Team Tuned In.'

I couldn't see where the cameras were positioned for the screens, but it zoomed out to include Jeanette's daughter in the shot. Jeanette's daughter looked like an identical, twenty-year-younger version of Jeanette with longer dark brown hair.

'Welcome Jeanette, and what's your daughter's name?' Casey asked from the stage. Jeanette placed the microphone in front of her daughter.

'I'm Lucy,' she answered in a soft voice.

Casey nodded and smiled at the two women. 'So, Jeanette, can you tell everyone here today what you want to create and manifest into your current reality?'

'I want to be able to make my small business successful again. It has taken a downturn over the past year, and I want to build it up again,' Jeanette said into the microphone.

'And what specifically does success look like to you Jeanette?' Casey asked.

'I run a small sewing shop and I want to be able to earn enough that I can hire more staff, so I don't have to run the business by myself anymore. I want to pay off my mortgage, buy a new Jeep and be able to take my family on a holiday for at least two weeks every year.'

The crowd started clapping around Jeanette. Her smile grew and her eyes started to well.

Casey joined in the clapping from the stage. 'How is that going to feel once you find yourself comfortably in that very position?'

Jeanette closed her eyes and smiled. 'It's going to feel like full-body tingles. As though for the first time in my life I can actually experience quality family time, full freedom and be able to provide, completely stress-free.'

The crowd roared for Jeanette, and Jeanette's tears started to fall. Lucy threw her arms around her mother, hugging her tight. The crowd quietened and Casey's eyes stayed locked on the mother-daughter duo.

'Jeanette, you've already taken the first step by conceiving this idea, writing it down, speaking out loud about the possibility of your dreams turning into a reality. You've also vocalised how it will feel once you achieve this goal—and it's only 9 a.m. By the time you walk out of here today, you're going to be another ten steps closer to your next reality. I can promise you that.' I watched Jeanette smile back at Casey on the screen. 'You're very lucky that your daughter introduced you to Tuned In, what a beautiful gift,' Casey continued. 'So, Lucy, tell us all the new reality you want to leave here with.'

Lucy's dimples deepened as the microphone moved back towards her. 'I'm currently in my last year of university to become a nurse. My dream job is to work overseas at the Royal Hospital of England. When I tell people this, they roll their eyes at me. They tell me how long it takes to get there. That I will have to spend ten years of my life proving my worth in Australia before I could even be considered for a role like that.' Lucy took a long breath, looking down at the ground, taking a moment to pause. 'But I feel that I'm meant to be there. I feel that I can score a job there still fresh out of university. I came to Tuned In because I really want to put everything into practice to make sure I find the right position and path to get there.'

I had never seen someone speak with so much passion about something before, Lucy was inspiring. The crowd clapped again, and I joined in on the applause.

'I love how you just said, *you can feel it* and that you *know* that you are meant to be there,' said Casey, smiling cheekily back at Lucy, like she knew the secret. 'I can sense it in your voice—a deep knowing—and I am on that path with you, Lucy. I can feel it for you too. I'm going to help you get even clearer and closer today. It won't be long before you'll need to purchase a plane ticket.'

The screens went black, and Casey strutted from either side of the stage, pointing to the upper seating level. The screens lit up with the image of a large man who looked to be in his early to mid-thirties. He now held a microphone from another volunteer.

'Hello Casey,' he said eagerly, giving Casey an emphatic wave. The crowd chuckled at his earnest enthusiasm.

'Hello there,' said Casey, 'what's your name?'

'I'm Joey. It's so great to be here and to be speaking with you. Wow, this is so exciting,' the cute chubby man said, clearly speaking his thoughts aloud.

'I'm so glad you're here as well Joey. I would love to know more about you. What brings you to Tuned In today?' Casey asked.

'I'm here because I want to lose forty kilos,' Joey said quickly, blurting out his words as if they were vomit. 'I've always been the yo-yo dieter who loses a big amount of weight only to gain most of it back straight away. I don't want to be that person anymore. From this very moment onward, it stops, because I know I have everything I need inside of me to achieve long-term results and I know that I am worthy and I deserve it.' Joey stamped his feet as he finished his sentence.

The crowd roared for Joey. I don't think I'd ever been in a room full of such open and confident people before, speaking their minds so clearly to thousands of strangers. These people seemed fine to me, as though they were already working towards achieving everything that they wanted. I didn't know what else Casey had to teach them. As far as I could tell Joey already sounded completely committed.

'I know that you already have everything that you need within you as well, Joey.' Casey smiled back at him, then continued, 'But tell me, why do you really want this? What is being forty kilos lighter going to do for your life?'

'My health and fitness need to be in the range to be able to finally live out my dream of joining the navy.'

'So, you're not just here to change your waistline. You're here to improve your health, live your dream and help the country by taking on a truly courageous role.' Casey kept her head held high to the top level on the stage, looking as though she had direct eye contact with Joey.

Joey's eyes drooped, he placed his hands in front of his heart in prayer and mouthed *thank you*.

I clapped along with the rest of the room and the screens once again went black. The blue light followed Casey along the stage as she made her way directly to the middle. She pointed into the audience, and I craned my head to see who she was pointing at. Within seconds, I was staring at my own face projected on the two screens.

I slowly stood up, my hands were shaking and my eyes wide, staring blankly into the shining light. A volunteer handed me a microphone and I instantly dropped it, feedback from the microphone sounded throughout the auditorium. I felt the crowd shudder as it sent a tingle down their spine. The volunteer handed me the microphone once again, this time I held onto it tightly with both hands, holding it against my chest. I felt the eyes of the entire room on me. At first, I couldn't look at Casey, I could only gape at my wide-eyed face staring back at me from the screen. I blinked a couple of times, pursed my lips and managed a small, tight-lipped smile. My eyes flicked back to Casey.

'Hello, beautiful,' she said, baring every single one of her perfectly straight teeth. 'What is your name and why are you here?'

Oh shit. This is actually happening. I took a deep breath, trying to reanimate myself as I put on my best stage face.

'Hi, I'm Daphne and I'm here to make an amazing man my boyfriend.'

I spoke confidently, following in the footsteps of the others who'd been in the limelight before me. I braced myself for the same round of applause, but it never came. I heard only a handful of claps and a couple of people cough.

'Make an amazing man your boyfriend. Who is this amazing man? Tell us a little bit about him,' Casey pressed.

'His name is Levi. We have been dating for a couple of months now and he is so amazing. He is the person who recommended I come here today.'

Casey smiled and stared directly at me. We must have been more than fifty metres away from each other, but I could feel her eyes locked on mine.

'What is it about Levi that makes him so amazing?'

I paused at the question, looking away from her gaze. Nobody had ever asked me that before. 'When I met him, I didn't realise that people like him existed. I've never met anyone who shares so many of the same interests as me. We vibe on everything together. He is so relaxed and successful and intelligent and fit and healthy and focused—he possesses everything that I want in a partner.'

'What is going to change when Levi transforms from someone you're dating into your boyfriend?' Casey asked me politely, but her face was still, her eyes stayed glued to me, I couldn't tell if she even blinked.

'When he asks me to be his girlfriend it will be proof that he is committed to me as much as I am to him. It's a commitment that says we want to do life together.'

'Have you thought about asking Levi if he wants to be in a committed relationship, first?' Casey continued to prod.

My eyes widened and I screwed my face up, completely forgetting that I was the focal point of the screens behind the stage. 'I would never do that,' I blurted out.

'Why not?' Casey asked innocently.

'Because that is not how I want things to work out,' I said, feeling my words start to speed. 'What if he says no!?' I shook my head. 'No, no, no. After this seminar, he is going to see how committed I am to everything that he loves and believes in, and I have no doubt he will ask me. That's the reality I want to create after this seminar.'

I ended my ramble with a shaky smile, remembering I was on the big screen this time. The crowd stayed silent.

'Daphne, have you watched much of Tuned In's content before? Have you checked out any of our social media platforms? Watched us on YouTube?'

'Honestly, no. I haven't seen anything. I'm only here because Levi has been to this seminar before, and he insisted I come along.'

Casey nodded. 'Levi is a smart man. I'm glad he told you to come here because, Daphne, today is going to be one of your most life-changing days. Today is going to move mountains for you if you join in and let it. Are you ready?'

I smiled and said with real confidence this time, 'I'm ready.'

The crowd roared.

'Great!' Casey said, walking back towards her stool taking a seat, keeping her eyes on me, gazing at me quizzically.

I passed the microphone back to the volunteer and dropped back down into my seat. Both girls on either side of me clapped and tapped my shoulder as if to say, *well done, you've got this!* I smiled at both of them politely. I picked up my pen and paper again, poised to write down everything that Casey was going to teach me.

Chapter 2

'For those of you who don't know, Tuned In is a community and education program all about the powers of manifestation. And that is exactly what we are all here for today. Many of you have experienced these seminars before and I am sure you have many stories of the magic you have cultivated from your learnings. If you haven't been to a seminar, I am sure you have dabbled in or experienced the magic of manifestation in your life through listening, watching, and reading the content on our platforms.

'Tuned In was created many years ago to equip people with the correct tools to manifest their greatest desires. I could tell you over a million stories of the wealth, health and love those members have cultivated from Tuned In's teachings. In fact, it was only a couple of years ago I was sitting in your very position at a TI seminar for the first time in my life. Since that moment, I was able to sell my small candle and soap business for six figures and live the life that I truly loved: joining Tuned In and travelling around the world teaching people how to dig deep, find out what it really is that their heart desires and manifest it into their current reality. I can honestly say that I am one of the luckiest people in the world today, thanks to Tuned In. It has allowed me to live out my dream life every day.' Casey sat on her stood in the middle of the stage waving her perfectly bouncy hair as she addressed the crowd from left to right.

'If you have never heard of Tuned In before, manifesting may be a completely foreign language to you, but it's not something to fear. I promise you, you are in the right place, and without even being aware of it, you have been manifesting everything in your life already. The saddest thing I find about being human, and the western society we live in, is that we don't truly know how incredibly powerful we are. To waste the magic inside of our very bones in the limited time that we have on this earth, shatters my heart. This is why I'm here—to awaken you to it and most of all, to empower you to utilise your own magic to achieve your potential.'

Casey took a sip of water. I scanned my eyes around the seats in front of me; she had every single person captivated, hanging on her every word. Casey placed her bottle back down on the floor and got comfortable on her stool.

'To manifest means to be clear or obvious to the mind's eye. It's simple really, what we believe, what we imagine, we can create. Daphne, where's Daphne?' Casey looked around the room and before I knew it the man with the microphone was standing in front of me again. 'Daphne, I'm sorry to pick on you, I'm just assuming that you may be one of the people in the crowd who has never heard of the word manifesting, would I be correct in saying that?'

I stood back up. 'Yes, that would be correct,' I spoke slowly into the microphone, looking down at the floor.

'Not to worry, you aren't the only one,' she said, brushing off my answer quickly. The volunteer disappeared with the microphone again and the screen re-focused on Casey's face. 'But whether you're a seasoned manifester or this is the first time you have ever heard of the concept, each and every one of you are here right now because you manifested being here. Whether consciously or unconsciously, at some point in your life, you thought of being exactly where you are right now.' Casey stood up from her seat. 'What I am getting at is, we are all the creators of our own life. Everything that has happened to you, whether it be good or bad, has happened due to manifestation. What I need you to completely know and trust with all your heart is that you are not the victim of your life. You are the creator! You can create the things that you want to bring into your life.' Casey screamed louder. 'Are you with me?'

The crowd screamed out 'YES!'

'Say it with me,' Casey continued. 'I AM THE CREATOR!'

'I AM THE CREATOR!' I screamed alongside everyone else in the room. I was almost shocked by how easily I'd embedded myself in this cultlike atmosphere.

Casey sat down and the audience quietened. 'Okay, so you might be thinking, all I have to do to get everything I have ever wanted is to just think it into existence. It's that easy, right?'

'Wrong,' a man's voice screamed out from the upper level.

Casey laughed into her microphone. Standing up from her seat, she started to slowly pace up and down the stage. 'Correct, it takes a lot more than just thought. If what we manifested became our reality by just a positive thought alone, think about all the things that we could have right now. But thought truly is one of the most powerful things when it comes to manifesting. The average person has approximately six thousand two hundred thoughts a day. Most of these thoughts run off subconscious patterns and belief systems that we might not even be aware we have. These thoughts mostly stem from our childhood and environment and stop us from having everything we want in life. They can stop us until the day we die if we don't listen to our true wants and desires. For instance, Lucy, I am going to use you as a shining example as I can tell that you are a student of Tuned In's work.'

The screens behind Casey quickly flicked to Lucy's smiling face. 'When we met Lucy earlier today, she told us about her dream job, and how everyone has told her she couldn't achieve something so big as a new graduate. If Lucy wasn't in tune with what she truly wanted, and not to mention her own personal belief system, she could have easily adopted other people's opinions as her own. Lucy might have spent the next ten years hoping to get to where she wanted to be, rather than stepping up and finding a way to get there herself, *now*. Lucy is already a step closer to manifesting her dream job into existence because she can now visualise the outcome. She believes she is worthy and isn't willing to let resistance hold her back. Manifestation is thought, but it also takes a whole lot of deep belief, passion and alignment.'

My head was in my lap, scribbling down words in my notebook, hoping that my scattered notes would make sense when I reread them tomorrow morning.

'To become an incredible manifester and start truly living your dream life, we need to break down the following steps.' Casey took a breath, while everyone watched on, enraptured, pens ready to take note. 'Number one: declaring what you want to create in your life. We can already tick number one off the list because you have already written down your intention.'

I followed Casey's instruction and drew a large tick next to *boyfriend* in my notebook. I smiled, feeling my heart flip looking down at the notes on my paper.

'Number two is identifying the beliefs that limit you. Your limiting beliefs are what have held you back from achieving your goal. Chances are, what you have written down is something that you have wanted for a long time, but you've found yourself not quite getting there, or other things have popped up in life, or you've given yourself excuses as to why you can't achieve that very thing. This is where some questions arise about your belief system and pushes us to step three—rewriting the rule book. Step three is all about transporting your own beliefs into your mind, and the real creation of what feels true and aligned to you, and starting to cultivate that within your consciousness. Step four is declaring the reality, knowing that you are worthy and stepping into the feeling of everything that you want. Not just thinking it, but visualising it, feeling it.'

Casey paused, bending down to drink from the glass of water that sat next to her stool. No head in the audience moved; like me, everyone was glued to their seats.

'Step five is about taking aligned action. We're going to put everything that we learn into an action plan on the steps that feel right for you. You're going to start taking these steps as soon as you walk out of the same doors you walked into this morning. Lastly, step six is all about surrender and knowing that you've done everything to align yourself with your dreams. From there, all you have to do is take a step aside and let your dreams come to you. Does anyone have any further questions or need more time with this?' Casey paused and scanned the room, but everyone stayed silent. 'Great, we all know exactly what we want—the hardest part is over. If you have any questions at any time, please put your hand up and someone with a microphone will come over to you. Alright, let's get into step two, limiting beliefs...'

The girl to my left nudged my arm. She looked different to the girl on my right—more corporate. Her long brown hair was slicked back into a low ponytail, and she wore black boots and a fitted black dress hidden underneath an oversized grey checked blazer.

'I'm getting a snack; do you want to come?' she whispered in my ear.

'Sure,' I said, placing my notebook and pen on top of my bag and tucking it underneath my chair. I stood up and followed the girl out of the row of seats and down the aisle while Casey continued speaking. At the back of the room was a black-clothed table filled with all my favourite types of food, the type of food that I tried to avoid the most. Croissants, chocolate chip cookies, muffins, and slices of all kinds of cake were scattered along the table in between bright platters of fruit. As we approached the table, a volunteer addressed us with a smile, her black polo emblazoned with a label that read, TI CREW.

'Can I get you ladies a plate?' she asked us both.

'That would be great, thanks,' the girl in the blazer said. We stood in silence until the woman came back with two plates filled with assorted treats and fruit.

'Thank you,' I said as she handed us a plate each.

'You can both take a seat here if you like.'

The volunteer gestured to some tables that had been set up for eating at the back of the room. We took a seat while Casey continued walking the crowd through the second step of the manifestation formula. I was interested in what she had to say; I wanted to walk away with as much knowledge as I could to take it home to Levi and show him how much I'd learnt. But I tuned out of Casey's spiel as I took a bite of the macadamia muffin on my plate.

'Mmmm,' I accidentally hummed aloud, tasting the sweetness in my mouth. It was a rare moment that I let myself enjoy sugar-filled treats.

'I'm Jessie by the way,' said the girl, not having touched her plate of food.

'I'm Daphne,' I said after swallowing a large bite of muffin.

'I know,' she said bluntly. I flashed her a tight-lipped smile, forgetting that everyone here now knew who I was.

'So, what are you here for, Jessie? What are you manifesting?' I asked, trying to make small talk in between muffin bites.

'I come here every year.' She leaned back into her seat and looked up at Casey on the stage. 'Work makes me come every year. I manage a creative studio not too far from here. Marketers, videographers, graphic design, you know, that sort of stuff.' I nodded, throwing the final piece of muffin into my mouth. 'The owners send me here so that I can bring the vibes back to the team.'

'Oh, that's awesome,' I said.

'Yeah, I'm getting paid right now which is great. Although after a while I feel like I've heard the same spiel over and over again, you know?' Jessie turned towards me with pursed lips, rolling her eyes.

'Yeah, I can understand that. Being a veteran, you must've manifested some pretty epic things into your life though, right?'

Jessie finally cracked a ghost of a smile. 'Yeah, I have, that's for sure. But I guess I'm kind of over the hype. Once you know that you really are in control of your life you don't need to amp yourself up this much anymore. You just go out and do it. You just get on the court and play the game how you want to play it. Do what you want to do and choose the path that you most desire.' Jessie took a bite of her cookie and waved a hand in the air, gesturing to the large audience. 'I guarantee you most people here are just going to use today to get high off the vibes and then go back to living their lives exactly how they were before they even walked through these doors.' Her gaze snapped from the crowd to focus back on me. 'That's why I don't like the hype.'

Jessie stared at me blankly. Her shrewd gaze made me feel a little uncomfortable. Although her face was expressionless, her eyes were watching me intently. 'I guess being a veteran also makes you aware of things that aren't going to work out,' she said.

I looked back at her a little confused. 'I thought the whole idea of this seminar is to learn how to bring anything you want into your reality?'

'Yes, but it also helps you separate between the things that you think you want and the ones that you *really* want.' Jessie set down her plate, but her eyes never left mine. 'It helps you realise what is truly meant for you. You can manifest anything, sure, but it doesn't necessarily mean it's going to be great for your overall life—sometimes we manifest hard times and lessons.

Not everything is sunshine and roses.'

I frowned. 'I don't think I understand what you're saying.'

She leaned towards me and placed an arm on my shoulder. 'Honey, I can save you the drama now and tell you that the man you're swooning over is not going to commit to you after today.' Jessie plucked a strawberry from her plate and took a delicate bite.

I felt the blood in my body rise from my heart to my head. Who was she to say that? She didn't know anything about Levi and me. Why say those horrible things here, at a place that preached nothing but good vibes? My mind raced with nasty thoughts about the girl in the blazer. I felt my face flush but Jessie simply stared at the stage looking as carefree as ever. She didn't seem bothered at all by her hurtful words.

'Why would you say that?' I asked her, practically snarling.

Jessie turned back towards me. 'I'm not saying it out of spite, I'm really not. Just trust me, you don't know it yet, but soon enough you will. There's something else out there for you,' Jesse said calmly.

I sat up tall in my seat and leaned in closer to her, trying to keep my voice down, making sure my anger wasn't going to garner the attention of the back few rows. 'Well, with all due respect you know absolutely nothing about Levi or me.'

'You're right,' Jesse said, 'I don't know either of you personally, but I do understand the situation. It's none of my business, but what you see in him and everything about him that you want to transpire in this world, will happen to you. It will happen to you in the most amazing ways. You just won't find all those things in an uncommitted man.'

My gaze returned to Casey; I watched her lips move on screen but I couldn't hear a word coming out of her mouth. I was too far in my own head, spiralling from a sugar rush and a rude stranger.

I took a deep breath and addressed Jessie for the final time. I put a smile on my face and spoke with as much politeness as I could muster. 'While everyone is entitled to their own opinion, I can tell you that after today, Levi and I will end up together— so thank you for your negativity and completely unsolicited advice, if you don't mind me, I'm going to excuse myself and learn everything I need to know so I can manifest this into my reality.' I jerked out of my seat.

'Have fun.' Jessie looked up at me with a grin. I tucked my chair underneath the table. 'Just remember the world is grey and round. We don't live on a linear, black and white plane,' she said.

I stormed off as quietly as I could without drawing the attention of the audience, or worse, Casey. *What the hell was Jessie talking about? We don't live on a linear plane? Please.* I took a seat and picked up my notepad and pen again. I took a deep breath and shook off the weird energy from Jessie so I could tune back into Casey's words.

'Now that we have become aware of what is really holding us back, we can rewire. We can say goodbye to beliefs that no longer serve us. It's time to rewrite our beliefs so that they serve us towards the next evolution of our soul and propel us towards everything that we can imagine in our future and bring it to fruition in our current reality.'

The crowd roared again, but this time I sat quiet. I must have missed an important part of the seminar while talking to Jessie. Now all I was focused on was the next couple of hours I had to spend sitting next to her. I glanced around but so far Jessie hadn't come back to her seat. I prayed she wouldn't.

'So, what I'm asking you now is what is missing from your own belief systems? What's holding you back from where you are now, to where you want to be in an hour, a day, a month, a year from now?' Casey stopped talking and I watched as her eyes scanned around the room until she landed on someone in the right-hand side of the front row.

'Hey lovely.' Casey beamed. The image of a thin young man wearing a red t-shirt and backwards baseball cap popped up the screens behind her.

'Hey, Casey.'

'What's your name, young man?'

'I'm Caleb.' He smiled a toothy smile; his blue eyes were strikingly attractive.

'Caleb, how are you enjoying the seminar so far? Is this your first one?' Casey settled onto her stool, folding one long leg over the other.

'It is my first seminar, and yeah, the energy here is great. To be honest, I was a bit sceptical coming here, but I am already glad that I decided to do this.'

'Ah, I love a sceptic.' Casey smirked. 'What exactly made you so sceptical about coming today?'

'I didn't want it to just be a jump around and "get hyped" day. And part of me was a little bit worried that I might be heading along to something that made me a part of a cult, but I can happily say that I am going to take away some good, tangible actions to implement into my life today.'

'Good, I'm glad we turned the sceptic around so quick; I think that's a record for me,' Casey smiled charmingly. 'So, Caleb, you must have a lot of things that you want to achieve to want to come along to Tuned In even though you were still sceptical?'

'Yeah. I guess I'm sick of wanting things and not having an actionable plan to achieve them. I'm a big dreamer and there is a lot that I visualise in my future. Not too long ago someone asked me if I would be happy if I was doing the exact same thing in five years' time and the answer scared me because the truth was no. I had so many ideas, but I wasn't actively pursuing them or making them happen. That was when I stumbled across your content and well, here I am.'

'Tell me specifically what your big dream is Caleb—what do you visualise in your future?'

'I'm an artist. I love to paint large canvases. I imagine myself having my own gallery one day with people coming to view my work. I imagine one of my paintings being the focal point of a person's house. I imagine people staring at it and it ignites their creativity and unlocks their deepest thoughts. I also imagine myself having my own gallery exhibitions across the world, but mostly around Europe... I know that's a fair way away,' Caleb admitted. 'I live pay check to pay check working in a factory and painting in the basement of my friend's house that he lets me live in at a cheap rate.'

The room was captivated by Caleb's story; he was so far from where he wanted to be but he spoke of his dreams with so much faith.

'I love how you didn't just tell me what you want, you told me why you want it too, how you want to make people feel. And I'm guessing you want it because of how much you love doing it too—you didn't mention that part though,' said Casey.

'Absolutely,' Caleb said. 'I couldn't imagine doing anything else.'

'I can feel that dream for you, I can see the authenticity shine through you when you speak about it. You are on the right path,' Casey said excitedly. 'Until you were asked that question you mentioned, did you have those visions for yourself?'

'I've always had these visions; I've always wanted them, but I guess I didn't think that someone like me would be capable of it. It was only until that moment and then stumbling across a video that Tuned In posted on Facebook that something small inside of me thought that it might be a possibility,' Caleb confessed.

'Can I ask you what you mean when you say, *someone like me*?' Casey probed.

'Well, I guess I wasn't really the kind of kid that you would expect to amount to anything much. I'm not someone that people would expect to have an art exhibition in Paris. I'm a child of the system. I only just scraped through school with my poor grades; I'm not the smartest guy. I don't have any family and I have spent a lot of my life on the streets. I've done a lot of stuff you're told you shouldn't do.' Caleb took a shaky breath, staring down at his feet. I was completely transfixed by this person baring their soul to a room of strangers. 'But I don't know… I just really love art. I love creating it, I love seeing other people enjoy it. Art is love to me.'

'Thanks for sharing all of this with us Caleb,' Casey said. 'But there's a couple of things you just said there that I want to be able to pick you up on and it should help you and everyone here today realise what I really mean when it comes to their belief system.'

'Sure, hit me with it. It's what I'm here for,' Caleb said, looking back at Casey wide-eyed. He stood slightly taller, stiff, waiting for her to hit him with the truth.

Casey looked around at the crowd. 'Okay, guys I want you to take all of this in and start thinking about your own scenarios and how similar belief patterns might be playing out in your own life.' I opened my notebook and flexed my pen. Casey focused back on Caleb. 'Caleb, what makes you believe that someone without a family, as you call it—a child of the system—will not amount to much?'

'I guess it's how you're treated young. Foster families, school teachers, the government, even in movies, kids like me don't really have anyone putting high expectations on us. I guess that's why I have never put them on myself,' Caleb answered.

'If you put all that aside for one second and I honestly asked you, is your art good enough to have its own gallery? Do you believe that people would come in and invest in your work?'

'Yes. I do believe it's good enough. I have a talent. I think that everyone is blessed with passions for a reason and that we have to pursue what we love. That's why we love it—we were born to do it. It was the team at Tuned In that taught me that.'

'So, what is it that's holding you back?' Casey asked.

'I guess it's everything from the past that has been taking up space in my mind,' Caleb said softly, muttering his last words.

Casey interrupted him. 'It's the fact that previously other people thought you wouldn't amount to much. But that has never been a part of your true belief system, has it?' Caleb shook his head and Casey continued. 'Because deep down you know your worth. Deep down you know that this is meant for you otherwise you wouldn't have this dream in the first place. You're right when you say we have dreams for a reason. We have our individual dreams and passions so that we manifest them and give them back to the world. So, Caleb, tell me, what is your new belief? What are you making a reality within your mind today so that you can introduce it into your physical reality in the near future?' Casey stopped talking and the whole room was silent, focused on Caleb's response.

He stood still, wide-eyed and emotionless. Eventually, he smiled. 'My belief is that it's going to happen. If I work hard enough this year, I can find myself some space to rent and it is going to be my first gallery. The first of many.'

The whole crowd clapped and screamed for Caleb. If he did make his dream happen, I'm sure he would have some very keen shoppers just from the room today.

'Okay, okay.' Casey gestured for the crowd to quieten down. 'I want every single person to look at the initial intention or goal you wrote down earlier and ask yourself, *why haven't I achieved this very thing already*? What specifically is holding you back?'

Everyone began furiously scribbling notes. I glanced back down at my handwriting.

I came today to make Levi commit to me.

Why hadn't he committed to me yet? I didn't know what was in my mind that was holding me back. I sat still, feeling blank while everyone around me seemed to be writing novels in their laps.

'And once you're clear on what it is that is holding you back, I want you to write down your new belief. Release the old and invite the new. What is the new belief that will skyrocket you closer to the life that you truly desire?'

I started writing, hoping things would start to make more sense on the page.

My new belief is that I am worthy of Levi's love and commitment. My new belief is that I am the one for him.

Chapter 3

Beep, beep, beep, beep.

I woke up sprawled across the king-size hotel room bed. I reached for my phone to press snooze but accidentally turned the alarm off. My home screen read 8 a.m. I threw it back down on the bed, letting my eyes drift shut again for just a moment longer. I didn't want to wake up yet. I couldn't be bothered with the drive. I stretched my body and let out a large yawn. *What a fucking day that was.* I was exhausted even though I'd slept like a baby the whole night.

Then my phone rang. 'No, not yet,' I groaned. I kept my eyes shut and fumbled around the bed to try and locate my phone again. I grabbed hold of it and opened my eyes. It was Levi. I jumped up in bed, took a deep breath and answered. 'Good morning handsome,' I said, trying to sound lively.

'Good morning, how are you?' his smooth carefree voice echoed through the phone.

'I'm great. I'm just sitting here about to start packing my bags and I'll probably grab some breakfast in the city before I start the drive home.'

'Nice,' Levi said. 'How did you find the seminar yesterday?'

'Honestly, I can't thank you enough for the recommendation. I think it was the most eye-opening, inspiring day I have ever had in my life. You just know about all the best things. I was actually just scrolling through Tuned In's Instagram page before you called, reading up on some of their stuff.' A little white lie didn't hurt anyone, and I *did* enjoy the day.

'Did you have any major breakthroughs?'

'Breakthroughs?' I questioned, wondering what he was alluding to.

'Yeah, did you get a clear idea about what you really want?' he asked.

'I did. You could say that I am manifesting some pretty wonderful things into my future,' I said coyly, hoping he wouldn't ask any further questions.

'That's great Daphne, I'm glad that you liked it… hey, the real reason I'm calling is because I wanted to see if you'd like to grab dinner when you get back tonight?'

I froze. *Oh my god.* Maybe Tuned In was real, maybe tonight was the night that Levi was finally going to ask me to be his girlfriend. Holy shit. I was an incredible manifester. This stuff worked fast!

'I'm home this afternoon,' I said, changing my voice again so that I sounded ever-so-casual, 'so dinner sounds great.'

'Perfect, meet you at St. J's at say, seven?'

St. J's was my favourite Italian restaurant. I loved that he picked it. 'Seven is perfect.'

'Great. I'll see you tonight Daph. Drive safe.'

'See you tonight.'

I hung up the phone, bouncing up and down on the bed. I couldn't believe this was finally happening! This was possibly going to be one of the biggest nights of my life. I had to get a move on and find something incredible to wear. Thank God I was in the city. I had enough time to pack my bags, check out, go shopping and get my ass back home to prepare for the rest of my life. I ditched my phone on the bed and dashed to the ensuite bathroom.

◆ ◆ ◆

'Where are you off to?' James, my housemate, called out to me as he walked past my bathroom, I looked down at the time on my phone, it was already quarter to seven.

'I'm just going to dinner with Levi,' I said, hoping that he wouldn't ask me too many questions.

'Is today a special dinner?'

'No special than any other, why's that?'

James loved to lecture me on life, and I was in too good a mood to listen to one of his philosophical rants.

'You just look really good, that's all.'

I glanced from the mirror to James, who was standing in the doorway of the bathroom. He shrugged.

'Aw thanks, James. That means a lot.' I smiled at him with my hand on my heart. I'd bought myself a new red one-shoulder bandeau dress for the dinner and it looked killer with my red vintage Louis Vuitton's—my treasured possession, that I miraculously found in a Lifeline store.

'Is he picking you up?' James asked.

'No, I was going to drive.' I placed my lipstick into my black handbag and stepped out of the bathroom.

'Where are you going to dinner?'

'St. J's,' I said, squeezing past James and into the hallway.

'Do you want a lift? I was just about to head into town,' he offered.

I paused and turned around. I loved the idea of a wine with dinner. 'Actually, that would be really great. Are you leaving now though?'

'Yeah, I was just grabbing my keys.' James jingled them in his hand. We trotted up the hallway and he opened the door for me. 'After you, milady.'

It was spitting lightly outside so we ran out onto the street and straight into James's blue Mazda hatchback.

'So, Levi's getting lucky tonight then hey...' James nudged me jokingly as he took off to the town's main strip.

I chuckled. 'Doesn't he always?'

'I guess so,' James laughed. 'When are you guys going to make it official?'

I flashed James a huge smile. I felt my stomach somersault thinking that I was only minutes away from the moment.

'Oh, that's why you're looking a little extra today. Tonight's the night! Are you going to put the hard words on him?'

My smile turned into a frown within seconds. 'Why do people keep saying that I'm the one that needs to ask? I don't want to be the one that asks, I don't think I'll need to. He knows how I feel. I'm sure tonight is the night that he is going to put the hard words on me without me even saying anything—I just feel it,' I rambled back to James.

'You don't have to defend yourself to me.' James laughed off my reaction. 'I understand where you're coming from. Sometimes guys just need a little push, you know? We don't always get all the hints or understand where we're going wrong. Asking for what you want in life is necessary sometimes.'

I pursed my lips pondering James's words and Casey's yesterday. James was right, I'm sure there was no harm in having an open conversation with Levi, but it was not how I envisioned it in my mind. Besides, after yesterday, it had never felt so real.

James pulled over right outside St. J's. I could see Levi sitting at a table through the large rectangle windows of the old brick building.

'Have a great night Daph. Just give me a call if you need anything.'

'Thank you.' I flashed one last smile at James and practically leapt out of the car. 'You have a great night too.' I closed the car door and ran towards the entrance, trying to avoid the rain.

'Hello, miss,' the waiter greeted as I closed the front door of the restaurant behind me. He must have been new. I was a regular at

St. J's, but I hadn't seen him working here before. 'Have you got a booking tonight?'

'Yes, I'm just with him,' I said, pointing to Levi.

The waiter nodded and stepped aside. I walked towards our table by the window. Levi was facing the back of the restaurant and hadn't seen me yet. I took a deep breath as I approached him.

'Hello handsome.' I smiled as Levi looked up at me from the table.

He stood up to hug me. 'Wow, you look gorgeous.' He held me and kissed my cheek.

'Thank you.' I took a seat and the same waiter who greeted me walked over to our table and filled up our glasses of water.

'Can I get you any drinks to start with?'

'I'd love a beer. Whatever local drop you have on tap,' said Levi.

'I'd love a glass of Pinot Gris.'

'Certainly.' The waiter nodded and walked away.

'So, how was your day?' I asked Levi, staring into his dreamy light blue eyes and admiring his long blonde hair that he'd tied back neatly for the occasion. He was wearing a white button-up shirt that he'd paired with some light khaki, slim-fit chinos. He looked great. I don't know if I had ever seen him wear blue before. It made his eyes shine beautifully.

'It was good, I got up early. The surf was incredible this morning, I ended up spending three hours out in the water and the swell. It's only going to come through stronger in the next couple of days so it's been a great atmosphere out there. Then I went into the shop to see if they needed any help, and I just sat in the office in the afternoon catching up on paperwork, but it was good. I think this week will be great for business since there's a lot of surfers heading to the coast from both ends of the state if the conditions stay how they are.'

I loved hearing him speak about his surf shop. He was so proud of it. He'd created quite a name for himself in the industry and had even started crafting his own fins.

'Oh and guess what?' Levi said as the waiter came back with our drinks.

'I'll come back over and take your order in a few minutes,' he said as he placed the drinks on the table.

'Thanks.' I smiled back at the waiter as he walked away. Levi took a sip of his beer. 'What's that?' I asked, steering the conversation back to his question.

'Johnny Cole is going to be using my fins when he goes to compete in Hawaii next month.'

'No way! That's incredible! How did this happen?' I almost screamed.

'He called the store and asked me! I've surfed with some of his mates before. They told him about my fins and how I am making them more sustainable and environmentally friendly. He said he was going to be up next week and asked if he could try them out, he's looking for some new gear for Hawaii. So, it's not one hundred percent yet—he might absolutely hate them— but I've got a good feeling about it.'

Levi's eyes were wide, his smile beaming. This was an incredible opportunity for him. I honestly didn't know too much about surfing, only what I gleaned from Levi. I wasn't a very good swimmer, let alone a surfer. But I'd heard him talk about this pro surfer, Johnny. Levi had always wanted to work with him. He must have manifested it.

I took a sip of my wine. 'You should have a good feeling about this, he is going to love your fins! Why wouldn't he? You're the best in the biz. I'm so proud of you!'

Levi smiled back at me. 'Thanks, Daph.'

The waiter walked back over and politely asked if we were ready to order.

We hadn't had a chance to look at the menu, but Levi and I

knew it like the back of our hands. 'Do you know what you want?' Levi asked. I smiled back, nodding. We usually rotated between three of our favourite meals. 'Perfect. I'll have the stuffed squid thanks,' Levi told the waiter.

'And I'll have the pumpkin gnocchi.'

'Wonderful.' The waiter smiled and then swiftly walked away again.

'Tell me more about Tuned In, how did you find it?' Levi asked.

'Honestly, I think it was the real positive boost that I needed in my life.'

'I'm so glad you liked it. I think sometimes recommending things like that can seem a bit cultish. Plus, I was worried if you didn't like it, you might have taken my recommendation the wrong way,' Levi said before taking another sip of his beer.

'What do you mean *the wrong way*?'

'Well, it can be a bit of a wake-up call when we become aware of how we have been acting or the things that are holding us back. It's confronting and it's not always nice to face, so I guess if you're not ready for it, it could seem like I'm trying to change you or that I think that there must be something wrong with you that needs changing. But I don't think that at all. I did recommend it to a friend once who came back and said exactly that. But something in me knew that you would love it and hopefully take on everything there is to learn with enthusiasm.' He paused to grin at me. 'I'm glad you've experienced it.'

'I thought it was a wonderful recommendation. Thank you.'

'Yeah Daph. I just think sometimes you hold yourself back from seeing the full picture of what you're really capable of.'

I took a sip of my wine, staring blanking into his eyes. I was unsure what he specifically meant by me 'holding myself back'?

'Tell me more about what you realised. What has it got you excited for? What are you now working towards in your future Daph? Tell me all the goss.' Levi smiled and leaned into the table, exposing his gorgeous left dimple. I wiggled in my seat and bit my lip, staring into his eyes. James's words ran through my head, *sometimes you have to ask for what you want.*

'I think the world just became clearer to me. I think I realised what's really important to me and what I see in my future,' I said.

Levi started laughing. 'That's the vaguest thing I've ever heard you say. It's okay if you don't want to tell me. I have no doubt that you're going to let everything you've learnt settle and go off and achieve great things.'

'Well… I don't know if I am going to go off and do them…'

'Oh yeah, you don't need to physically go anywhere. You have amazing contacts here; everyone loves you. They love what you do—you're freaking incredible. All the girls in town talk about you and your style. Now it's your time to believe in yourself and spread your wings a little wider,' said Levi, raising his voice with excitement.

'The stuffed squid and the pumpkin gnocchi.' The waiter appeared again with our meals and placed them on the table in front of us. It was such quick service. I looked around the restaurant and realised there were only two other couples out dining. This place was usually packed but I supposed the rain had kept people at home.

'I'm a little unsure what you're talking about,' I said honestly.

'Sorry, I'm just guessing you made some career aspirations yesterday and I'm getting excited for you, that's all.' Levi picked up his cutlery, tearing his squid apart with his knife and fork, looking at the food as though he hadn't eaten all day.

'What do you mean career aspirations?' I asked as he took a bite of his squid.

'Well, you don't want to be a stylist in someone else's store forever.'

'I love my job?' I frowned. Even though the smell of fresh gnocchi invaded my nostrils, I sat still, neglecting my cutlery.

'I know you do. I think you're so talented. I just thought you'd come back from yesterday wanting to do more with it. I'm not having a go, Daph,' he clarified in a rush. 'I'm sorry, I was just getting excited for you.'

My heart dropped and my hope for the night was beginning to fade. Maybe I did just have to be straight up and ask for what I wanted. If you can believe it into existence, it can happen, right? I had nothing to lose.

'What I worked on creating and so-called manifesting yesterday had nothing to do with my career or my job. It was about what matters to me the most: my relationships. The people that matter to me.' My voice started to drift off and I could feel a lump in my throat. 'I guess I focused on you,' I said, picking up my wine and taking a long, nervous sip.

Levi chewed down another piece of his squid. He stared at me, probably sensing every inch of my fear. 'What do you mean Daph?' he asked softly, leaning in towards me.

I placed my wine glass back down on the table. 'Well… I focused my manifestation on my relationships. My intimate relationships. And you, the possibility of our future.'

I held his gaze as I finished the words. He stiffened, blinked and looked away.

'As in, me and you as a couple?'

'Yes. As in us together, finally, in a committed relationship.'

There was no going back now. I couldn't believe he looked so shocked. Not a single part of him expected this conversation. My heart sunk even deeper. This is not how I imagined my night would turn out. I'd been yearning all day for these carbs and I wasn't even hungry anymore.

Levi sat his knife and fork down on the table. He placed his elbows on the table, clasping his hands underneath his chin and leaning in closer. 'I wasn't expecting this.'

'What do you mean you weren't expecting it? We've been

dating for months now. Dinners, sleepovers, morning coffees, I always come and watch you surf. We're practically a couple, aren't we? We know everything there is to know about each other…' I heard my voice climb higher and I sat back, looking around the restaurant to check if anyone was looking at us. I took a deep breath and another gulp of wine.

Levi reached for my hand across the table. 'Hey, I'm sorry. I guess it's just a complete shock because you've never said anything about it before. You've never once mentioned you wanted a relationship. You've never spoken about it. You've always been so chill with our current friendship that I thought that was all that you wanted. So, I guess I never questioned it anymore.'

I pursed my lips and nodded, looking away, hoping the tears forming in my eyes wouldn't drop in front of him. 'So, you're saying all this time you've never once thought of me as more than a friend?'

'I respect you completely. I love the time that we spend together—you're an amazing chick. But if I'm completely honest, I guess I've never considered this being a relationship because I haven't wanted one. I thought this was a perfect set-up because it seemed like we were on the same page.'

I pulled my hand away from Levi. I couldn't look at him anymore. 'I think I'm going to go,' I muttered, standing from the table. I couldn't be in public right now. I couldn't be around him. I didn't want to embarrass myself any further, I couldn't keep the tears back any longer. I felt one spill down my cheek.

'Hey, no, Daph. Sit. Let's chat about this. You haven't even touched your pasta.' Levi stared up at me wide-eyed.

I picked up my handbag. 'No, I have to go. I can't be here right now,' I said, choking back a sob.

'At least let me call you an Uber.' Levi went to grab my hand again, but I yanked it away before he had the chance.

'No, I'm fine. I'm going.'

Without a second glance, I walked swiftly out of the restaurant. It was as though every single emotion that was humanly possible was causing a fever in my body. I couldn't even feel the heavy rain pour down on me as I walked down the street. I had to get past the restaurant and out of Levi's sight before I could let the wave inside me crash. I walked two buildings down, feeling my red dress cling tighter to my body, drenched from the rain. I turned up an alleyway and crouched down to the concrete floor in my heels. My tears fled down my face, lost in between raindrops. I couldn't breathe, I felt suffocated by the pain, unsure if I was about to vomit out my heart.

Chapter 4

'Daph... Daph... Daph.'

I looked up at Lisa from the front till, she was standing still in the middle of the shop floor. 'Yeah?'

'Are you okay? I can cover for you this afternoon. Give yourself some time. You can head home early.' Lisa looked at me, concerned. I glanced at the time on the register. It was 1 p.m. She was due to knock off and I only had another hour before I had to close the store anyway.

'No. I want to be here. You go home,' I insisted. 'I'm sorry if I've been so off today, I'll be back to my full self on Monday, I promise.'

I don't know why I promised that. I had no idea how I was going to feel. I couldn't even process my current feelings. It was like I wasn't even here, as though I was a ghost, spaced out and numb, just watching the world happen around me. I couldn't stop the constant image of his eyes flashing through my mind and a fresh wave of pain reminded me I was still here and everything I wished had been a dream from the night before was still very much real.

'You don't need to apologise,' said Lisa. 'You know who should apologise? Levi, for being such a fucking dick!' Lisa's voice rose as she stamped her feet on the floor. She caught herself, looking around to make sure there were no customers in the store.

I laughed. 'The coast is clear.'

'Seriously though, who on earth does that guy think he is? You guys are perfect together.' Lisa walked over towards the counter. 'You do realise he is going to try and get you back though. There's always a moment that hits 'em and they finally realise that they just lost the best thing that ever happened to them. Promise me you won't take him back. Let him suffer. If he can't see your worth now, don't give it to him later, it will be too late.' Lisa sounded more savage with every word. I was almost worried about what she would do if she ran into Levi in the street.

'I don't think he is going to come back,' I replied softly, feeling my heart ache as I spoke the words.

'He will, they always do. But you'll be miles away, doing amazing things when that happens. Things will only go up from here baby girl and you're going to be travelling in leaps and bounds.' Lisa raised her voice and her arms with a little too much enthusiasm for my broken heart.

I forced myself to smile back at Lisa. While I appreciated her motivational speech, I sure as hell couldn't feel that way right now. If anything, it made me feel sick. Sick about the day I spent at Tuned In, sick at Casey; how dare that strange woman make me spend money on some seminar that perpetuates the idea that we can have everything we want just by imagining it. If anything, yesterday taught me that the exact opposite was true.

'Are you sure I can't help you with anything else Daph?' Lisa's eyes dropped towards me, like a puppy dog vowing for love.

'I'm sure. Get out of here and go enjoy your Saturday afternoon,' I said, opening the front door and holding it open for her. I didn't want her to spend the rest of her afternoon consoling me, I just wanted to be alone.

'Thanks, girl,' Lisa said as she headed out the door. 'I'll see you on Monday. If there's anything you need in the meantime, you know I'm only a call away.'

'Thanks, Lisa.'

She reached out and hugged me, then turned out of the shop and walked down the street. I gave her a quick wave and stepped back into Duskk. Once inside, I collapsed into the large showroom chair. I sat there, frozen, lost in a whirlpool of my thoughts, retracing moments with Levi. I kept reliving the past like a movie in my mind. In hindsight, if I knew it was going to end exactly the way it did, what would I have done differently? Could I have changed the outcome? I shook my head and took a deep breath, staring at the large clock on the wall behind the front counter. It was near closing time. After another minute, I crawled my way out of the chair and began to close the store.

I locked the front door and made my way up the street. What was I going to do tonight? Saturday afternoons usually ended with me walking over to Levi's store to help him close up for the week before grabbing a drink by the beach. I'd have to find a new way to spend them now. As I walked aimlessly towards my car, I stopped and peered in the window of Lady Meyers, my second favourite designer store, after Duskk of course. The mannequin in the window was dressed in a cream strapless jumpsuit. My god, it was divine. Their new season collection must have just landed. I hesitated on the street, knowing full well if I walked in and tried on the jumpsuit my bank account was going to resent me for it.

If only it was free.

I couldn't help myself. I wanted to feel the material on my skin. I deserved a little pick-me-up.

'Hey girl, how are you?' Lillian called out to me from behind the counter as I walked into the store and straight over to the new season collection.

Lillian was a young girl, new to retail and studying fashion. She was probably my main competitor in the town when it came to styling, but I didn't see her that way. She was lovely, and it was great to know someone as passionate about fashion as myself.

'I just unpacked the new collection this morning, and when I saw the jumpsuit, you were the first person I thought of,' she said as she approached me.

I smiled back at her. 'You know me too well. I couldn't stop staring at it in the window.' I reached out and felt the linen material on the coat hanger. 'Oh my god, it's amazing.'

'I know right.' Lillian plucked the jumpsuit from the rack. 'I'll pop one in the change room for you.'

'How much is it?' I asked as I trailed behind her.

'Free,' Lillian said as she hung it up in the nearest change room.

I laughed. 'Funny. Seriously, how much is it?' I'd already fallen in love with the material without even trying it on, and I was already finding ways to justify what would be an extravagant buy.

Lillian looked confused by my comment. 'Daphne, it's free.' She looked me straight in the eyes; she was serious. But her stare was blank.

I paused for a moment, waiting for her to tell me that she'd punked me, but her face never changed. I lifted the jumpsuit from the hook and handed it back to Lillian. 'In that case, I don't need to try it on. I'll take it,' I said, adding a nervous laugh to the end of my sentence, waiting for Lillian to tell me the real obscene price.

Lillian took the jumpsuit out of my hands. 'Perfect. It's going to look so incredible on you anyway! I'm sure you're the exact person that they had in mind when they were making it.' Lillian walked over behind the counter and carefully wrapped the jumpsuit up in light pink tissue paper before placing it in a Lady Meyers bag. I walked slowly over to the counter, unsure about what was happening. Were there hidden cameras? Were there police around the corner ready to arrest me for stealing?

Lillian held out the bag with a smile. 'There you go.'

'Lillian are you sure?' I stood still, analysing her blank face.

'I'm not sure but if I put myself in the shoes of the designer then yes, you would have been the exact girl I was thinking of when I made this. So, where are you going to wear it?'

'I… I don't know yet.' I finally reached out and grabbed the bag out of Lillian's hands.

'Are you heading out tonight?' Lillian asked. She'd started to potter around the store, moving clothes and creating an even distance between each item that hung on the racks to ensure the store looked perfect.

'I wasn't planning to,' I muttered.

'Well, now you've got a perfect excuse to head out. If you wear the jumpsuit, take a picture for me, will you?' Lillian asked. 'It would be great for our socials.'

'Sure, Lillian.' I smiled back at her and walked to the exit. 'Thank you.'

'Have a great weekend.'

Outside, I stood agape on the street. *What the fuck just happened?* I looked down at the bag that was in my hand and back up at the mannequin in the window. *If only it was free…*

My body broke out into goosebumps as I stared at the headless plastic body dressed in the linen I'd fallen in love with just moments ago. I shook my head and laughed out loud, staring at the bag, still unsure if this was Lillian's lame version of a practical joke. Nevertheless, I continued along the street with a hell of a lot more spring in my step than before.

'Mum, can I get chocolate and strawberries on top of mine?' A young girl with curly blonde hair nagged her mum as they walked ahead of me into the frozen yogurt shop. I felt my stomach rumble thinking about chocolate coconut frozen yogurt.

If only it had no calories, I would eat a little bit of it after work every single day.

I halted outside the door of the frozen yogurt store. I wonder…

I walked straight through the door and picked up an empty tub from the counter. I strutted past the young girl and her mum and headed straight for the chocolate coconut frozen yogurt machine. I pulled the small lever and filled the tub with delicious dark swirls. Once it was almost full, I shuffled over to the counter where a red-haired girl in a frozen yogurt visor stood.

I placed my tub down on the scales. 'How many calories are in this?'

'Is it chocolate coconut?' she asked.

'It is.'

'Our chocolate coconut frozen yogurt is calorie-free,' the girl said with a bright smile. I felt a warm rush throughout my whole body, as though a force of energy was pumping through me, a power I'd never felt before. *Wow, I would love calorie-free Oreos.*

'And what if I add crushed Oreos on top as well?'

The young girl smiled wider. 'Our Oreos are calorie-free as well.'

'I'll top it with Oreos.'

'Certainly.'

The girl walked away and topped up the tub with Oreos before handing it back to me. I paid, then walked out of the store with my tub of calorie-free frozen yogurt in one hand and my Lady Meyers shopping bag in the other. I felt the rush of energy flood through my body again. The feeling started in my chest, radiating warmth around my heart then to the top of my head, and through my fingers and toes. However, it strangely felt like I was in control of it. I took a deep breath. Feeling a little overwhelmed, I sat down on the gutter outside of the frozen yogurt store and had my first taste of calorie-free frozen yogurt. I couldn't detect any difference.

I sat and ate the chocolatey goodness while staring mindlessly towards the street. I had to tell someone about this. No one would believe me until they physically saw it for themselves. I took the final bite of yogurt and crunched down on the last of the Oreos before I set down the tub and picked up my phone. Before I could even call Amy, my phone buzzed in my hand and her name appeared on my screen.

'Amy,' I answered.

'Daph, are you okay? James just told me the news. Why haven't you called me? Do you want me to come over? I'll bring over some dinner and wine?'

My heart sunk again as my thoughts snapped back to Levi. For a minute there I'd almost forgotten.

'No, actually... I want to go out. Let's grab dinner at the Balcony tonight. I'll call Lana too.'

'I'd love that.' Amy perked up through the phone. 'Are you sure though?'

'Absolutely. I have an amazing new outfit I want to wear,' I said, and a smile took over my face as I stared down at the bag beside me.

Chapter 5

'Daphne!'

Amy stood up from our usual outdoor booth at the Balcony as she saw me enter the room. It was my favourite Saturday night hang; a relaxed yet fancy rooftop bar and restaurant that showcased the best views of Byron Bay. Amy held her arms out to embrace me in a tight hug before pulling away and looking me up and down.

'Wait a minute! Are you wearing the newest Lady Meyers? I saw a preview of their new collection on Instagram—I didn't even know it was released yet. How did you afford that? Did you get a promotion? Or are you drowning your sorrows in debt? Because I'll tell you now...' Amy spoke so rapidly. Lana sat back in the booth laughing as she watched Amy's mouth motor. Lana stood up and darted in front of Amy to give me a hug of her own, effectively cutting off Amy's ramble. Lana was wearing a gorgeous short orange silk dress, while Amy wore a black crop and a long white linen skirt like the material of my jumpsuit. We always seemed to match our outfits.

'You look amazing,' Lana said. 'We bought you a marg.' She pointed down to three fresh margaritas on the table.

'I love you guys.' I grinned, took a seat opposite my two best friends and enjoyed a long first sip of my margarita.

'What I was going to say before you cut me off Lana.' Amy jokingly narrowed her eyes at Lana. 'Is... fuck that guy.' She raised her margarita and said, 'So long loser, here's to hotter, more committed men.'

'Here, here,' I replied as we clinked our glasses together.

'But in all seriousness girl, how are you?' Lana asked.

'Honestly, I don't know how I feel. After the... you know, break-up I guess happened... things have been crazy.'

'What happened?' Amy asked. 'James called me today to tell me that it was over with you and Levi, so I just called you straight away.'

'Honestly, I'm shocked. I thought you guys were perfect for each other,' Lana chimed in, then quickly added, 'You don't have to tell us the story if you're not ready to talk about it yet.'

'No, I need to tell you everything.' I took another sip of my margarita and got more comfortable in my seat. 'Have you heard of Tuned In?' I asked the girls.

Amy nodded. 'Yeah, they're like a cult self-development kinda thing, right? I've seen their videos pop up on my Instagram a couple of times.'

'To be honest, I'd never looked them up before. But on Thursday I ended up going to the city for one of their seminars because Levi recommended I go,' I explained.

'Ohh, I get it now,' Amy said. 'Red flag. Levi's a bloody cult lover.'

'What's Tuned In?' Lana asked, furrowing her brow.

'Okay, I need you guys to keep an open mind.' I was slightly nervous to explain all the events of the past couple of days.

'Has Levi brainwashed you?' Amy asked bluntly. She glared at me wide eyed, sipping down on her margarita straw as though it was a slurpy.

'No, well... not Levi. I don't know. Just let me tell this story...' The girls leaned in closer, awaiting my gossip. 'The Tuned In seminars are about how to manifest. Essentially, it's about how to materialise everything that you desire into your existence. They teach you the steps to make your thoughts your reality. I left really believing that Levi was going to officially ask me to be his girlfriend and that we would end up together. When Levi invited me to go to dinner on Friday night, I was almost certain that he was going to ask me. Instead, it went the complete other way.'

I watched Amy's nostrils flair, while Lana shook her head sadly. 'So essentially that prick brainwashed you and then dumped you. Ugh, that makes me so mad. Doesn't he realise what he is missing out on? You're one of the most beautiful and talented people I know.' Amy rolled her eyes and crossed her arms.

'I guess he just didn't really see me as more than a friend. Not to mention the seminar felt like a complete waste of time—getting my hopes up and believing so strongly that it would happen only to have my heart torn apart. Fuck, it hurts.' I released a shaky breath, grateful to be surrounded by the two people who meant the most to me, even if there was a chance, they might think I was insane. 'But then this afternoon something really weird happened. When I left work, I was walking past Lady Myers when I spotted this very jumpsuit.' I placed my hands on my stomach, referring to my outfit. 'I thought, wow, it would be so great if it was free. I walked in to try it on and when I asked how much it was, Lillian told me it was free. I walked out of the store with this very jumpsuit for FREE!' My voice grew louder as I explained what had happened. 'I had the thought, and it became true. I manifested it.'

Lana and Amy shot each other a dubious look.

'Maybe Lillian just gave you the suit for free because she wanted you to post a couple of pictures in it on Insta,' Lana said.

'Yeah, if anything, it's great business for her if the town's best stylist is wearing clothes from the store she works in,' Amy said. Her wide eyes made me feel as though she was assessing my mental wellbeing.

'Absolutely, I couldn't agree more. But then I thought I would test it out again. I walked past the frozen yogurt shop thinking how great it would be if my favourite chocolate coconut flavour had no calories. So, I went inside and poured myself a tub, and when I went to the counter and asked the girl working there how many calories it had, she told me chocolate coconut was calorie-free frozen yogurt,' I said intensely.

Amy looked at me again, this time even more concerned. 'I think she was just having a joke with you Daph.'

I continued, undeterred, 'But then I thought it would be great if the Oreos were calorie-free too. And when I asked her how many calories the Oreos had in them, she said zero!'

The girls still look unconvinced. 'Daph, you've had an emotionally intense couple of days. Are you sure you're okay?' Lana replied.

'I'm serious guys, I'll show you. What would you like me to manifest right now?' I still didn't understand what had happened today, or even how I'd done it. I didn't know if it would ever work again but I had to at least try in front of my friends to prove I wasn't going crazy.

Amy drained the last of her margarita. 'You can manifest us another round of margs,' she joked.

'Okay fine.' I looked down at Amy's empty glass sitting on the table.

I'd love another round of margaritas right now.

I felt the warmth flow through my body again, burning my heart, tingling my spine and almost vibrating outside of my body. The girls narrowed their eyes, observing me curiously.

'Excuse me, do you ladies like chilli?'

The question came from a tall man with shoulder-length brown hair at the end of our booth.

Lana sat up straighter in her seat. 'We love chilli. Why's that?' I watched her smile and stare into the man's intense green eyes. He smiled back at her with perfect, white teeth. He wore a pair of fitted black jeans that were slightly ripped at the knee and an oversized motley crew t-shirt. He wasn't Lana's usual type of guy.

'I just ordered a round of margaritas for my friends, but the bartender stuffed up and made them all chilli ones. We just wanted the OG. I noticed your empty glasses; would you like them?'

'Ah, hell yes we would like them,' Amy said.

'Perfect, I'll bring them over.' He flashed another grin at Lana. 'I'm Jack by the way.'

'I'm Lana,' Lana said, butting in before anyone else could introduce themselves first. 'And this is Amy and Daphne.'

'Lovely to meet you ladies, I'll be back.' He slunk away from the booth and back inside towards the bar.

'What the fuck,' Lana said.

'Thank you, do you believe me now?' I asked.

'Could be a coincidence,' Amy said. 'But who cares? If this really does work, we're going to have to hang out even more often because I could do with some more free margs and designer clothes in my life.'

'No guys. Didn't you see Jack? Don't you have any idea who he is?' Amy and I looked back at Lana with matching blank stares. 'Jack is the bass guitarist for The Koras,' she said in a raised whisper, barely holding back a scream.

'Lana, I had no idea you were such a muso. Who knows the bass guitarist?' I asked with a laugh.

'I looked them up earlier today because I knew they were playing in town this weekend.'

'Yeah, I forgot about that,' Amy said. 'I tried to get tickets months ago when the show was announced but it sold out in minutes.'

'Can use your newfound powers to get them to have a drink with us?' Lana asked eagerly.

'Oh, so now you're on board with it?' I jibed.

'Girl, you just got us free chilli margaritas, do your thing!' Amy insisted.

'Well, in that case, I can't wait to hang out with The Koras tonight and watch their gig from backstage—and I also can't wait for Jack to place those delicious lips of his right on yours, Lana.' I finished my sentence with a click of my fingers, laughing to myself, pretending that I was magic. Within seconds, I looked up and Jack was standing there with a plate of chilli margaritas.

'Hey ladies, I know you're probably just enjoying a nice girls' night out, but I don't suppose you would like to join my friends and me for dinner? It's just not every day you run into three gorgeous girls like yourselves.' Jack's words were a little corny, but I knew the answer was going to be a *yes*.

'We'd love to,' said Lana, as she stood up from the booth.

'Great,' he said. 'We've got a private room out the back.'

'Perfect,' I said.

Amy and I stood up in unison, following Lana and Jack back behind the bar where a private blue door opened for us.

My whole life I'd lived in this town and visited The Balcony as soon as I turned eighteen. We spent most weekends here, but I had never been into the private function room. One wall was made entirely of glass, overlooking the beach. The sun had almost set and the last rays lined the horizon, beaming through the room. In the middle of the room was a large white table with gold cutlery and crème napkins.

'Lads meet the ladies. Ladies meet the lads,' Jack announced.

We sat down, scattering ourselves amongst the empty seats. Amy was opposite me, her eyes wide as she mouthed, *what the fuck? How are we here?* I was feeling the exact same way but for just a moment I decided I wouldn't question it. For tonight, I just wanted to let whatever happens, happen. After the events of the past couple days, I just wanted to be with my girls, having fun.

Making memories that we would laugh about for months to come. I looked around at the other seats where four other men sat.

'Hey ladies, I'm Eli.' A guy with scruffy brown hair and green eyes almost as intense as Jack's was sat next to Amy. He looked like the emo kid in the band. His nails were painted black, and he had a look on his face that read *hot danger*. Amy turned to her left and caught his eyes.

'Hey Eli, I'm Amy.' She flashed him a heartbreaking smile. 'I like your t-shirt.' Eli was wearing a navy tee that read *The Koras* in white across the front.

'Thanks, it's my band,' he said cheekily back to Amy.

'I figured. And what is it that you do in your band?' Amy flirted back.

'I'm the drummer,' Eli said, leaning back in his chair proudly.

'Maybe you'll have to show me your sticks sometime.' It was a classic Amy line.

Lana and I both laughed. Her eyes peeled on Jack, smiling coyly. Everyone took turns introducing themselves and we learned that Eli was Jack's younger brother. Then there was Matty, the guitarist, a stern-looking guy with chocolate brown eyes and a short ponytail. He wore a red t-shirt that had the words *try me* printed across the chest. The Koras' manager was Nolan, the oldest of the bunch, who introduced himself by saying, 'I'm not in the band. I'm just with the band.' It was clear he'd made the joke at least a dozen times before, but I chuckled out of politeness.

The lights dimmed as the sun set completely and the room doors swung open. Two waiters walked in carrying six plates between them and set the food down on the middle of the table.

'I hope you don't mind, we already ordered food before you came in. There should be something here that everyone likes though,' said Jack.

'I love the whole menu here. This is so great—thank you so

much,' I replied to Jack. It looked as though they'd ordered the whole menu. The waiters left and reappeared again with more food. Edamame, sashimi, bao, chicken wings, fries, and dumplings covered the table.

'I am so hungry, this all looks amazing,' Lana said, selecting something from every dish and filling up the gold-stained plate that sat in front of her.

'Can I get you any more drinks?' one of the waiters asked the room. I took a sip from my chilli margarita, almost forgetting that it was there until the waiter mentioned more.

'If you could just make sure that our glasses are always full that would be really great,' Eli said.

The waiter nodded and began clearing the empty glasses.

'Oh, you're my kind of man Eli,' Amy said, flirting shamelessly.

'I like your jumpsuit, Daphne,' the man to the right of me said. I turned to look at him as I filled my plate up with dumplings.

'Thank you. Sorry, I didn't get your name?'

I knew exactly who he was. He was wearing tight black pants and his blonde hair was spiked in all directions. He wore an oversized white t-shirt with a wild, colourful print on the front, the kind that tricks your brain into thinking it's moving if you focus too hard on it. But I was more focused on the intricate fine-lined tattoos that dressed both of his arms. He was the lead singer of The Koras and he had the voice of a rockstar angel.

'Sorry, I'm Kas.' Kas leaned over to grab the plate of chicken wings and put some onto his plate. 'It's Lady Meyers, yeah? It looks as though it was made for you.'

I balked. 'How do you know that?'

'How do I know it's made for you? You got me there,' he said with a chuckle. 'It's just how it looks on you.' I laughed, feeling my cheeks glow pink. It also felt a little coincidental that he was saying the exact same words as Lillian had said earlier today. I took another big sip from my drink.

'No, I mean, how did you know it was a Lady Meyers?' I clarified.

'Oh, she's good friends with my sister.'

'She? As in, *Sophia Meyers*?' Sophia was the designer of Lady Meyers. She was incredibly talented—I would have given anything to work alongside her as her stylist. 'Wow, that's amazing. I love her stuff. She's on my list of people who I really want to work with.'

'Are you a designer too?' Kas asked in between bites.

'No, I'm a stylist.'

'Oh, that's awesome. Well, I'll introduce you to Sophia someday. She's really great,' he said casually.

I froze in my seat, but my insides were doing cartwheels. *Did he actually just say that?* 'That would be great.'

He smiled back at me. 'Yeah, no problem.'

I would love to style something alongside Lady Meyers.

'So, what were you lovely ladies out for tonight?' Jack asked all three of us across the table. 'What did we rudely interrupt?'

I looked at both Amy and Lana opposite me, hoping that they wouldn't mention the fact that we were out to debrief about my recent broken heart.

'We're just celebrating life,' Amy said. 'It's a girls' night. We're just having margs, celebrating us.' Amy dazzled the room with her smile. The waiter reappeared carrying a large tray of drinks and placed one in front of each of us.

'So, you didn't have any other plans tonight?' Jack asked.

'No, we were just going to have dinner and see where the night took us,' I replied.

'I think after dinner it should take you to our gig,' Kas said, turning to look at me.

'I don't know, are you any good?' Amy joked back.

'Well, I guess you'll all have to come along to find out,' Eli replied.

'We're in,' Lana added.

'Well cheers ladies, here's to a fun night. Welcome to The Koras' tour,' Eli said.

'More like, welcome to the girls!' Amy butted in, 'I think you're in for more of a wild ride with us.' I smirked at Amy.

'Well, in that case, I can't wait,' Eli said. He raised his glass and we all clinked ours in the middle of the table.

'Alright guys, I hate to ruin the party, but you boys do have to be at the pre-meet-and-greet in half an hour so eat up,' Nolan said.

'Yeah boss.' Matty, who had stayed quiet most of the night, saluted Nolan and everyone filled their plates up one more time.

'So, other than each of you being musicians, do we get to learn anything more about you all?' Lana looked across the room as she dived into a plate that looked like my favourite eggplant dish on the menu. I held my hand out for Lana to pass the plate across to me once she was done with filling her plate. She didn't miss a beat.

'Knowing that we're musicians is one more thing than we know about you girls. Tell us something about yourselves,' Eli jumped in.

'Maybe we like mystery,' Amy replied with a wink and a sultry smile. She was about the only woman in the world that could pull off a move like that and still have it ooze sex appeal.

'Offtt. Well, in that case, I think you're our kinda girls.' Eli smiled even wider than Amy. The tension at the table was palpable.

'I think I need to go to the bathroom.' Amy stood up from her seat and met my eyes with an intense glance.

'I'll join you,' I replied, standing up. 'Is there a private bathroom in here?'

'I'm afraid not honey, just the main ones outside,' said Eli. Amy and I made a swift exit and as soon as the door closed behind us, she grabbed my hand, stormed across the bar and pulled me into a large unisex disabled toilet. She locked the door.

'DAPHNE!' Her eyes were wild. I knew this look; she had an idea and she wanted me involved. Amy always had fun ideas, although they weren't always the greatest or safest. 'Do you realise what is happening right now?!' I could tell Amy wanted to scream but she was speaking under her breath, trying not to draw attention to the fact there were two people locked in the bathroom.

'Yes, we're having dinner with The Koras.' Though my tone was calm, I was anything but.

'You created this! You made this happen.'

'Not completely, I had no idea that they were going to be here tonight,' I said. 'Did you actually need to pee?'

'No,' she said pacing up and down the small bathroom. I took a seat on top of the closed toilet lid. 'I just needed to talk to you about this. I just needed to understand this. Firstly, I know I joked with you earlier, but without your so-called power, I would not be sitting next to the hottest guy on earth tonight, ready to bang him!' I couldn't help but giggle at Amy, she loved the glitz and glam, anything that was associated with fame and fun. Amy was the one friend of mine who was always up for anything.

'This wasn't my power. I seriously had no idea that they were even in town.'

'Maybe not completely, but if it weren't for you, Jack may never have brought drinks over and I really don't think he would have invited us all to have dinner with them and go to their gig!'

'True,' I drawled, still a little unsure how I felt about my new 'so-called' power.

'What I'm saying is, it feels like you can literally make anything happen for us immediately. This is crazy!' Amy started to scream under her breath.

'You think this is crazy? Try being me right now!'

'Are you serious, I would kill to be you! Do you know all the things that I would have done already if I was you?'

'I can imagine,' I said with a smirk.

Amy laughed. 'Okay, but seriously, girl, we really need to start using this to our advantage. We could have anything we want! There are no restrictions.'

'There are no restrictions that we know of.' I couldn't get too excited yet, it was all too surreal.

'Daph, seriously, you used your powers to look like a boss ass babe in that Lady Meyers jumpsuit and flirt with Kas from The fucking Koras.' She raised a perfectly manicured brow at my expression. 'I saw you guys getting all cosy before. Imagine what else you could create for your life. You could style the biggest names, meet the most influential designers...'

'Kas knows Sophia Meyers,' I blurted.

'As in, the woman who made that very piece of perfection you're sitting in right now?' I nodded, feeling the butterflies rise in my stomach as Amy continued, 'GIRL! Now is your time. What on earth are you doing sitting on a toilet seat?'

'You literally dragged me in here.'

'The rest of your life awaits!'

I paused and stared at Amy. I bit my lip and then broke out into a smile. She was right. I deserved this moment after my recent humiliation. Now all I had to do was go out and get absolutely everything I ever wanted.

'God, you're so right!' This time I did scream back at her with excitement.

'I know, I'm always right.'

Amy flung the bathroom door open and we ran out excitedly. 'Also, I would really love a Louis Vuitton bag and to spend the night with Eli,' Amy said as we walked back through the bar towards the private room.

'You are not going to need help with the latter.'

Amy grinned. 'So, you'll get me a bag?'

'I'll get you a bag and a pair of shoes,' I answered dutifully.

'I am so glad we are best friends, always remember I loved you even before your crazy powers.'

Matty opened the door just before I placed my hand on the doorknob. 'Are you okay girls?'

'Yeah, sorry we took so long,' I said as the whole crew filed out into the restaurant.

'Are you ready?' Kas looked up at me smiling. 'Don't worry there will be more food and drinks backstage at the venue.' He flashed a cheeky smile at me. Lana walked out the door, stood in between us and threw an arm around us both.

'Let's go girls,' Lana whispered as we reached the top of the stairs.

Chapter 6

'How do you get kiwi berries at your gig? Do you know how hard it is to find these?' Amy said, picking up the small green berry and popping it in her mouth.

'They're on our wager. Sometimes it's nice to flex you know,' Eli said with a laugh.

'Can I add to your wager?' she replied, nibbling the berry.

'That depends. How many shows are you going to stick around for?' Eli winked and walked on stage to meet with the rest of the band who were doing their sound checks.

Amy re-joined us with a glass of pink gin in her hand. She sat down opposite us on the three-seater leather couch, plonking herself comfortably in the middle and crossing her legs. She took a long sip from her glass then turned her eyes onto me, leaning in.

'Okay, make it happen Daph,' she said, straightening up and taking another long sip.

'Make what happen?' I squinted my eyes at her and picked up my margarita glass from the coffee table. I sat in between the two large leather black chairs that Lana and I'd made ourselves at home on. We were sitting in the so-called 'green room'. I'd never been backstage at a gig before, so I didn't know what the average green room looked like. But to me, this seemed excessive.

But it was the excessive luxury that I was excited for tonight. The possibility of another moment like this was rare and I was glad to have Amy and Lana experience it with me. Men and women dressed in black continued to walk in and out of the right-side door of the green room, pouring drinks and delivering plates of fruit, cheese, sweets and cured meats.

A woman dressed in black with a long blonde ponytail peeking out the back of her black cap approached us. I blinked at her twice— she looked so much like one of the women passing the microphone around at Tuned In. Was she following me around? Did she know how I got this so-called power?

'Can I get you ladies anything?' she asked in a soft, polite voice.

'No, I think we're fine,' Lana said.

She smiled back at Lana. 'Well, if there's anything that you need at any time, I'm your girl. I'm Issy the way.'

'I'm Lana, this is Amy and Daphne,' Lana introduced us.

'Hey, Issy...' I started, still wondering if I should ask her more about who she was and if she was at the conference on Thursday.

'Yes?'

'What exactly is your job here?'

'I'm a full-time tour manager, or a personal assistant I guess you could say. Nolan is the main manager of events, but I'm the right-hand woman who makes sure that everything runs smoothly and there's no drama.'

I smiled and nodded. If her full-time gig was to manage The Koras' tours, then she wouldn't have time to be an assistant at any esoteric self-development seminar. She had enough on her hands. I sat my drink back down on the side table and shook my head. Maybe I'd drunk too much tonight if I was already thinking that a girl dressed in black was going to save me from some sort of incredible magical ability I'd somehow acquired.

'Hey Issy.' Amy flashed her signature toothy smile back at her. 'If it's not too much to ask, I would just love it if we could keep these margs coming all night. That would be amazing.'

'Of course.' Issy smiled back at Amy. 'I'll make sure your

glasses are always full.' She snapped up Amy's empty glass and dashed off to get her a refill.

'Anyway, what was I saying?' Amy leaned in closer to us again, her eyes wide. 'Daphne, Lana, I think that we should make this current experience last a little bit longer than a night.'

'What do you mean?' Lana asked, narrowing her eyes.

'Did you hear Eli before?' Amy's voice raised slightly in excitement. 'He asked how many gigs I was staying around for. We could ride this night for weeks. Daphne, make it happen.' Amy was getting even more carried away than usual and all I could do was laugh. 'I'm serious. I've never been more serious in my life.' Amy reassured us. 'You know those moments that you get in life that just feel so right, the moments that you know you are going to replay in your mind forever—the one that you would relive over and over if you could. For me, that's right now. *This moment.* Except this time Daphne has somehow turned into a real-life fucking fairy that can make anything happen and I may get to experience this moment over and over again for real! We're hanging out with The Koras, guys! I was born to be famous, even if it's only as a groupie.'

I laughed out loud again at Amy. She was fully embracing this moment, and hell, I wanted to follow the journey with her. I had no idea how long this power was going to last, and I had to make the most of it. I picked up the glass from the side table and took another sip, clouding my judgement just a little bit more.

We're joining The Koras on tour.

'We're going to party with The Koras for as long as we want,' I said, raising my glass. At that moment, Issy returned and handed Amy a fresh margarita.

'Between you and me,' Issy said as she took the empty glass from my hand, 'I hope you do. I could do with some more female company around here.' She smiled brightly and walked away.

'Wait be careful, do we really want this?' Lana butted in.

'Too late now, I bet you little miss magic over here has already made it happen,' Amy said with a wide grin.

'We can't follow them around on their gigs. I'm on prac, I'm so close to finishing my degree,' Lana said, being the usual voice of reason that our friendship group needed.

'Umm... let me check,' Amy said as she pursed her lips, looking over into the distance, holding her hand to her chin. 'Oh yep. I'm available, I quit my job right now.'

Issy returned and promptly placed a fresh drink in my hand. I took a sip, chuckling at Amy. My drunken giggles were in full force. I knew how much Amy hated her job. She spent her days as an admin assistant at a local real estate agency, daydreaming about the moment she would get discovered on the street by a talent agent. I wasn't even quite sure what specifically wanted to do but Amy was born for the stage. 'Come on Lana, I know you work hard and love what you do and all blah, blah, blah, but you've studied for years, take a few weeks off would you!'

Amy's eyes didn't leave Lana's. Lana worked incredibly hard; she was fast-tracking her degree in nursing. She was incredibly passionate and dedicated, but Amy was right, I couldn't remember the last time she'd taken time off for anything.

Lana shrugged. 'I guess you're right. My boss has actually been begging me to take some of the annual leave I've accrued.'

'See!' Amy almost squealed. 'And Daph, thanks to he-who-shall-not-be-named, the girls at the store would understand that you need some time off. It's the benefit of working in a woman-lead business—heartbreak leave is a thing.'

I took another large sip of my drink, inhaled deeply, and nodded back at her.

'Fabulous.' Amy smiled and held out her margarita to toast one another. We clinked glasses and cheered. 'I think we're about to have the most fabulous time of our lives!' Amy shrieked with excitement.

The Koras had just returned to the green room and Eli came straight over to the couch, placing his hands on Amy's shoulders and lightly massaging them.

'Can I make it even more fun?' Eli leaned in, looking down at Amy.

'Hmmm,' she hummed under her breath. 'That depends on what you're offering.'

'Well...' Jack said as he walked over to us, with Kas following close behind him. Both men took a seat on the armrests of mine and Lana's leather chairs. 'We think you girls are great. You have no idea how hard it is to come across a group of fun carefree ladies when you're constantly on the road. I know this is super forward, so don't feel pressured, but we were all wondering if you would like to join us for the next couple of gigs.'

We all shared a look. *It was really happening.*

'Where are they all?' Lana asked, looking up at Jack.

'We're currently on a tour of the country, most capital cities and a couple of small towns in between. Everything will be paid for since you would be our guests. We do work a lot and there are some recording sessions and a lot of media in between gigs. I'm sure you all have important jobs to get to that you can't put on hold for a while, but, I don't know, we just wanted to extend the invite. It would be really great having you all there while exploring new places. We do work a lot, but there's sights to see, new restaurants, unlimited drinks.'

'Guys, I'm going to speak on behalf of all of us right now— we would love to. Thank you so much for asking us, we're honoured,' Amy replied sweetly. I studied her face, she smiled softly and gracefully, but with the look in her eyes that made me unsure if she was going to cry or scream from barely concealed excitement.

Lana nodded along with Amy's words, and it prompted the largest smile I'd seen on Jack's face so far. I felt a squeeze on my shoulder—it was Kas. I smiled up at him. My god, his eyes were divine. Although my heart was in pieces at the thought of Levi, I could still appreciate Kas's incredible energy and intense eyes.

'Are you going to join us?' he asked softly.

'Absolutely.' We shared a smile.

'I think your friend's right, I think this is going to be a really fun time.' I nodded at Kas's words and almost jumped out of my seat as I heard Eli scream.

'SHOTS!'

We all looked up at him and Issy appeared carrying a tray with a large blue and white ceramic bottle, shot glasses and lime wedges. She placed the tray on the table between Lana and me. I watched Issy pour eight glasses with practised ease. Nolan and Matty appeared, both standing on either side of the couch. Issy handed everyone a shot and a wedge of lime.

'What is this?' I whispered to Kas, but before he could answer, Eli jumped in.

'This is our pre-show tradition, one shot of the finest tequila there is just to get the juices flowing for another amazing night. So, cheers everyone. Let's make this one to remember.'

'Here, here,' Amy said.

We all raised our glasses, tipped back our heads and drowned the shots in one. It was the smoothest tequila I'd ever had in my life—I didn't even flinch.

'Here's to the first of many!' Jack declared.

Issy made quick work of collecting our glasses and lime peels before disappearing again.

'I'm so excited to see you play; we all really do love your music,' Lana added. I looked around the room, observing the five faces of the band members and their manager. It was clear that they appreciated Lana's comment, as if it weren't something they'd already heard thousands of times before.

'Thanks,' Kas said. 'We hope you like the gig.'

'Okay guys, half an hour to stage time,' Nolan jumped in.

Kas squeezed my shoulder again and I looked up at him. 'Okay we've got to go and get ourselves ready,' he told me.

'No worries,' I said, flashing him a smile. The boys walked out of the green room and down a hallway. It could have been a dressing room or a drug den for all I knew. I turned back to Lana and Amy.

'Wait. Do we even know where their tour is?' Lana asked, staring blankly at Amy and me. It was clear her mind was caught somewhere between *oh my god, I'm so excited* and *is this a good idea?* I was usually the one that sat between Lana and Amy— Amy as the go-getter, wild child and Lana as the voice of reason.

Before either of us could reply to Lana, Issy reappeared. This woman seemed to be everywhere, always popping up at the right time. 'Sorry, I didn't mean to interrupt. Nolan just mentioned that you lovely ladies will be joining us for the remainder of the tour.'

'How long is the tour?' Lana asked.

Issy took a seat on the couch next to Amy, resting a clipboard on her right knee and holding a pen in her right hand.

'Our Australian tour is only for another three weeks, but there's a show almost every night. We have a lot of travelling coming up. Flights and long drives. We have to fly to Melbourne mid-morning tomorrow for a couple of days. Are you all okay with that?' Issy's tone was casual as if she'd repeated this conversation many times.

'Yes, that's okay with all of us,' Amy quickly replied and then shot a glance to Lana as if to say, *don't say anything. Trust me, it'll all work out.* I knew these girls inside out; one look gave away everything.

'Great. I'll just need some personal details from you all and I'll book your tickets right away. Tomorrow's flight is at 11.45 a.m. I'll make sure that you all have plenty of time to head home and pack a bag though.' Issy passed the clipboard and pen to Amy so we could start filling in our details. 'Do you have any other questions about the trip?'

'I can't think of any at the moment, but if we do, we'll let you know,' I said.

'I have one question,' Amy began, passing the clipboard along to Lana without filling it in. 'What's it like on tour? Do you like the travelling life? Are you always organising flights for random groups of girls to tag along?'

'I haven't organised flights for a group of girls before, other than some of the boys' previous girlfriends. This is a random experience. The past couple of weeks the boys have been travelling around Asia and I've overheard a couple of conversations about how they wish they had a better crew of people to travel with, maybe experience more than the inside of music halls and partying with hardcore fans. They aren't the most wholesome people when a party gets involved. I've seen some things, believe me.'

'I bet you have,' Amy butted in with the biggest smile on her face, hoping that Issy would spill some more gossip.

'But honestly, they all have hearts of gold. If you're up for an adventure, to travel around, have fun and enjoy music, you'll have a great time. And who knows, if you love the Australian tour so much maybe you'll want to join us for the upcoming American one.'

Lana skipped right over me and handed the clipboard back to Issy. I noticed that she'd filled in my details *and* Amy's as well as her own. I smiled. She was great with that sort of thing.

'I'm excited,' Amy announced.

Issy stood up and took all our glasses. 'I'll be back,' she said, and once again swiftly disappeared to top up our drinks.

I sank back in the chair and took a couple of deep breaths, staring back at Amy and Lana's disbelieving smiles. I placed my hand on my chest, feeling my heart flutter. I didn't know if it was from too much alcohol, my shock at our current situation, how quickly things had changed in my life in the past seventy-two hours or seeing the elation on my two best friends' faces about the spontaneous adventure we were about to embark on.

'I guess we're doing this,' Lana said. 'I'll let my boss know I'm finally taking annual leave first thing in the morning.'

'Yes, girl!' Amy almost screamed. 'All of this right now, it's all part of the adventure. When your best friend becomes some sort of magical manifester, you have to jump on that wave with her and ride it all the way to the shore of a private island.' Amy's eyes widened when she heard her own words. 'Oh my god, can we? Can you magically get us to an incredible private island?'

I laughed. 'One thing at a time please.'

'Yeah, you're right. Let's just see how these guys turn out and maybe we can make that our next wish.' Amy smiled and placed her hands across her forearms and nodded like she was in *I Dream of Jeannie.*

The smell of fresh, woody cologne filled the room, and I looked up to see that The Koras had reappeared, with Kas leading the way. He flashed me a half-smile.

'It's go-time!' Eli jumped up and down from behind him.

Amy stood up from the couch too. 'GO GET 'EM BOYS!' She wiggled her hips and threw her hands in the air.

Eli walked straight up to Amy, leaned over the back of the couch and placed his right hand on her cheek. He tried to whisper but I could still make out his muttered words. 'And straight after, I'm going to come get you.' He flashed Amy a sexy smile and she giggled before he rushed off to join the guys side-stage.

As they walked on, we heard the crowd roar; it must have been packed out there. 'Let's go watch,' Amy said.

Issy returned with a fresh round of margaritas and directed us to where we could watch the show. We couldn't see the crowd, so I guessed that they couldn't see us. The band had just begun playing 'In My Mind', one of my favourite tracks. Eli smiled broadly at the crowd as he hit his snare drum, while Matty and Jack strummed their guitars and nodded along to the beat. Kas was in his element as he worked the stage, serenading the crowd with his powerful angelic voice. I caught myself smiling uncontrollably, lost in his electric energy. Singing along to the lyrics.

'It's always been you on my mind.
Every day, never apart.
The memories of you restart my heart.'

Chapter 7

I woke up to the faint sound of Lana's voice and a hand on my shoulder, rousing me from sleep. Where was I? I opened my eyes. Lana was knelt in front of me, smiling widely, and holding back fits of laughter. I was curled up on the black leather chair. Had I fallen asleep? I blinked a couple of times then sat up slowly.

'What happened?' I croaked. In the corner of the room, I saw Amy and a couple of the band members lingering around a table of food, laughing about something Eli had just said.

'How are you feeling? Are you okay?' Lana said, her smile wide and eyes glassy. Every second word rolled on her tongue. How much had she had to drink?

'The last thing I remember was watching the band.' I leaned closer, trying to whisper, hoping I hadn't made a drunk mess of myself. 'What did I do?'

'Don't stress, you didn't do anything embarrassing. I think you put yourself to bed, or at least asleep, curled up in this chair. Did you spew though? I was a bit worried you spewed.'

'I have no idea. I literally don't remember a thing.' I sat staring blankly at Lana. I wasn't a stranger to having too many drinks, but not recalling what I did was new. I hoped that as my brain awoke, my memories would soon come back.

'We were all watching the band play from side-stage, Issy was doing a fantastic job of following Amy's orders,' Lana said with a wry smile. 'The drinks kept flowing, I had to stop. I think you may have just had one too many because you left to go to the bathroom. I thought you needed to be sick but when I came back in to check on you, you were curled up asleep.'

'Oh, thank god.' That did sound pretty accurate. There was always a moment where I knew I'd had too much to drink on a night out or at a friend's party. I was a classic smoke bomber, leaving to take myself home to bed. 'I just remember drinking so much. I hope I didn't make a fool of myself.'

'Not at all.' Lana smiled back at me warmly. 'How do you feel now?'

I sat up taller, stretching my arms and rolling my neck, trying to shake off the last of my nap. 'Good, I think. Maybe a little scattered. What time is it? Did I miss the whole gig?'

Lana laughed. 'You did miss a lot of it, but don't worry there will be another one tomorrow night.'

That's right—we had agreed to travel with the band.

'I think it's close to 1:30 a.m. The gig finished about an hour ago and we've just been hanging out here for a bit.'

'Great, so you've all been partying around me while I slept?' I asked, picking at my fingernails.

She laughed again. 'Something like that. Don't worry you weren't snoring.'

'That's comforting.'

I saw Kas slowly appear from behind Lana. He took a seat on the couch opposite me. 'Here she is, sleepy beauty,' he said as his eyes met mine. I blushed. Lana stopped kneeling and took a seat beside Kas. 'Was our gig that bad that it put you to sleep?' he said cheekily.

'I remember enjoying the gig, and the margaritas perhaps a little bit too much.' I was too embarrassed to banter back with him.

He smiled and let out a short laugh. 'Yeah, I think we've all had enough to drink tonight. We're going to call it an early one.'

Early? I wondered how long The Koras usually partied after their gigs.

'We're all staying at a hotel down the road. I think Amy is coming to stay, I don't know if you are Lana?' Kas looked to Lana and she nodded back at him. Kas returned his gaze to me. 'You're more than welcome to come and stay as well. Or we can get Issy to give you a lift home?'

Before I could reply, Amy—looking as drunk as ever—and Eli appeared in the corner of my eye on the opposite side of the room, wrapped in each other's arms.

'DAPHNE!' Amy shouted. 'I'm so glad you're awake.' Amy giggled in between slurring her words. 'We're going to Sync now. We'll catch you in the morning!' They turned and stumbled off together before anyone could say goodbye.

'You're staying at Sync?' I piped up with a little more energy, looking back at Kas.

'Yeah.'

Sync was the newest hotel in Byron. It looked incredible from the pictures I'd seen on Instagram from the influencers who got to stay there. It was an old Mediterranean-styled building with the main property for hotel rooms and private villas attached on either side. I'd always wanted to see what the rooms looked like in person, but I could never bring myself to book a hotel that was well beyond my budget and only ten minutes from my house. But the décor and interiors lit up my inner designer.

'Well in that case, I'd love to come stay.' I was too excited to ask if they had a villa or a hotel room. *I'll let it be a surprise.*

Jack walked over and dropped down on the couch next to Lana, throwing a casual arm around her. She leaned into him, smiling easily. Lana seemed so happy, so relaxed—not worried about anything. Honestly, it was a little unusual for her.

'Are you ready to go?' Jack asked.

I looked back up at the table where everyone was standing

moments ago, but the room was empty. We were the last ones. I stood up quickly, stretched again and let out a yawn. Kas stood up in front of me and held out his hand out for Lana, helping her off the large couch.

We made our way out of the green room and down a hallway towards the back door. The security guard bid us goodnight and we meandered up the main street with Jack leading us toward the hotel.

We arrived at Sync only a few moments later. It was covered by a tall white rendered gate, so no one from the street could even try to peak in. The only touch of paradise an onlooker might see were the tops of the palm trees that towered behind the gate. Jack pulled two room cards out of his front pocket and swiped one to open the gate.

The front garden was lush and green with old-fashioned cobblestones carved down smoothly for anyone wearing stilettos—a godsend for Lana and me. The palm trees were in full view now, framing the arched doors that stood before us.

'Here you go mate,' Jack said, handing Kas a key. Jack took Lana's hand and walked towards the arched doors. 'See you in the morning.'

Lana sung as she swayed into the building behind Jack, 'Sweet dreams.'

'You too.' I waved at her as they disappeared behind the dreamy doors.

I felt slightly panicked; I wasn't expecting to be left alone with Kas? Had I been too naive?

'Do you want to come with me?' Kas said kindly, taking my hand. I nodded. We steered away from the front doors and followed the stone walkway along the right side of the building. I looked up at him, then surveyed my surroundings again. I felt like 1 should pinch myself. The night hardly seemed real; wearing my favourite designer, staying at a hotel I'd only dreamed of. *You manifested it, Daph.*

We turned the corner around the other side of the building, and I was greeted with the sight of five white-brick, Mediterranean-style villas, each separated by a couple of meters, boasting front balconies and gardens. Some had small frangipani trees, others had grass trees and even though it was dark, I was sure I saw a tree with mangos or maybe peaches. I'd have to double-check when the sun came up.

'Sorry, we're not in the main building. I just have a one-bedroom villa,' Kas said.

'You don't need to be sorry about that.'

I wanted to laugh—he seemed so sincerely sorry about the fact that we weren't inside the main building, but the villas were my real dream. Kas led me towards the second white hut and dropped my hand so he could swipe us inside. We walked down a large, open hallway with timber floorboards, and halfway down the hall was an old white dresser that blended with the crisp, white walls. On top was a taupe vase filled with white roses and greenery. Next to the flowers was a note and an unopened bottle of Moet champagne. The note read, *Enjoy your stay in Villa 2, Wildflower. Decorated perfectly for the go-getters, wanderers and curious kinds.* I was in the right place, I'd never felt more at home. I picked up the bottle of Moet. I felt refreshed after my sleep and a short walk in the cool night breeze.

'Does everyone who stays here get this?' I asked Kas, still holding the bottle. 'Or do you just get it because... you're you?'

Kas closed the door behind him and shrugged his shoulders. 'I don't know.'

'Well, I'm going to have a glass,' I declared, trotting down the hallway, realising I was yet to take my heels off. The hallway opened to the main room, and I hovered in the archway, taking it all in. 'Wow. This is exactly how I imagined it.'

A large king-size bed with a cane bedhead and two matching

side tables were the room's centrepiece, propped against a peach-coloured wall. The bed was dressed in crisp white sheets and to the far side were two glass double doors, which led to the balcony. A small kitchenette with big white cupboards, peach splashback tiles and a small, round cane dining table sat in the second room.

With the champagne bottle still in one hand, I fetched two flute glasses from the kitchen cupboard and brought them to the bedroom and set them down on a side table. I finally kicked off my shoes, scooted back on the bed and uncorked the Moet with a loud *pop*. Kas watched me with a soft smile. There had only been a few times in my life that I was able to enjoy a glass of one of my favourite bubbles. There was no way I was going to let another opportunity pass me by. I filled the glasses and held one out to Kas. He kicked off his sneakers, took his glass and settled onto the edge of the bed. I wiggled closer and propped myself up next to him.

'Well, cheers to you,' I tapped my glass to his and took a sip.

'Why cheers to me?'

'Um... I don't know, cheers to another gig then, cheers for this Moet and cheers for letting me experience Sync.'

'You're welcome.' Kas took a sip of his drink, staring blankly towards the end of the bed. 'Do you think this is weird?' he asked, angling his head towards me.

'Do I think what's weird?' I asked, before indulging in another delicious sip.

'That you're here. I don't know. You're different, you don't seem super stoked to be here?' His eyes narrowed in on me.

I sat up taller on the bed, leaning into the pillow behind me. 'What are you kidding me? I can't believe I'm here right now, getting to experience this gorgeous place.' My voice got louder with every word. I wanted to make sure Kas knew how much I was truly grateful to be here.

Kas fixed me with another blank stare, then let out a huge laugh. 'That exact answer is what I meant. You're not a groupie in the slightest.'

I looked back at him wide-eyed, unsure if this was his strange version of a compliment.

He placed a hand on my knee. 'Oh, I didn't mean that in a bad way—and not that there's anything wrong with groupies either. I'm not trying to jump you or anything, believe it or not, I'm not actually like that. It's just... it's refreshing that you're not either. You don't actually want anything from me.' I watched his eyes move around the details of my face as if he was trying to figure me out.

I gave him a shaky smile. 'I guess this situation is a bit weird. But a lot of weird things seem to be happening in my life lately. I don't mean to be so forward, but why did you invite me here then? If you knew I wasn't some hardcore fan? You hardly know me.'

'Maybe that's why I invited you... I don't get much time to spend with actual genuine people.' He moved the pillow behind him, getting more comfortable as he drank more champagne. 'So, Daphne, tell me something I don't know about you, other than the fact you're an amazing stylist.' He looked straight at me.

I blushed a little at his comment. I made quick work of refilling our glasses, avoiding his gaze.

'What would you like to know?'

Kas giggled alongside me. 'Have you always lived in Byron? It's really beautiful—well, from the little I saw of it when we flew in this afternoon.'

'Yep, born and bred here. Lana, Amy and I have been inseparable since high school. It is a beautiful town though. I'm lucky I guess; I've never wanted to live anywhere else. I've just always wanted to make things work for me here. It does give me this warm, homely feeling. I did move away once when I went to fashion school. I lived in Brisbane for two years. It was a great experience, but I wanted to come home.'

'So, the dream is to have your own styling business or designer store here?' Kas probed.

I paused, now staring out at the end of the bed. I knew what my usual answer for this was: I would usually reply with something like, *no, I'm so happy with my job and my life, I wouldn't have it any other way.* But after the wakeup call with Levi and now talking about it with a stranger at 2:30 in the morning, I knew it was total bullshit.

'Yes,' I replied strongly. 'I want to have my own styling studio that will also stock my own designs and those of my favourite designers.' I'd always dreamed about this, but I was paralysingly afraid of failure. I spared a glance at Kas—he was smiling.

'Yeah, I can see that for you.'

'Thanks,' I said. 'And what about you? Surely, you're living the dream right now.'

'Yeah, I am. I'm lucky, I guess. We got picked up young. We've been touring for almost four years now and each gig just keeps getting better. Every time I walk off that stage or I leave the studio, I think how much I really couldn't imagine myself doing anything else.' Kas relaxed, sinking deeper into the pillow as he polished off his second glass.

'How old are you?' I abruptly asked.

'I'm 25,' he said. 'And you?'

'22.'

He nodded. Kas set his glass down on his bedside table. 'Is there anything else you'd like to know about me before we sleep next to each other?'

'No, I don't think so.' I yawned and placed my glass down next to the champagne bottle. 'As long as you're not a snorer, we'll get on just fine.'

It felt wrong the minute the words left my mouth. I'd only said it because Levi used to snore. I hadn't slept next to anybody else in a long time, and I'd never slept next to someone I had just met. I mentally tried to shake all thoughts of Levi.

Kas laughed, oblivious. 'That, I can confirm.'

'Oh, I just realised that I have nothing on me to sleep in,' I said shyly.

'It's okay. We can get your stuff in the morning. Would you like to borrow a shirt?'

'Yes, please.'

He walked towards his suitcase that was sitting in the far-right corner of the room and handed me a large t-shirt. I padded off to the bathroom and quickly shut the door behind me. I peeled off my jumpsuit and sat down to pee, realising I was a little bit dizzy for the second time tonight. I looked at the jumpsuit on the floor and Kas's shirt that I'd dropped down next to it. I finished up, washed my hands and threw on Kas's shirt. I studied my face in the mirror; my make-up was a mess; my cheeks were pink and my black bags from now two nights of little sleep were on full display. I scrubbed my face clean before stepping back into the bedroom.

Kas had already tucked himself into bed and turned off the lights. I tiptoed over to the bed, lifted the blankets, and tucked myself in. I lied flat on my back, breathing deeply. On my left, Kas was out cold, snoring ever so quietly.

Chapter 8

The next morning, Kas was nowhere to be seen, but I woke up to Lana standing over me and Amy sitting on the bed beside me. I took a moment to come to my senses.

'I didn't realise you were such a deep sleeper,' Lana said. 'We're making a habit out of trying to wake you up.'

'Sorry, it was a late night. What's the time?' I asked.

'A late night hey?' Amy nudged me as I sat up in bed. 'Tell me everything!'

'There's time for that later, first, you really have to call someone from your work.' Lana stared at me wide-eyed as she handed me my phone. I was still a little dazed as I took it—I couldn't even remember where I left it last night.

'Have you called yours?' I looked back at Lana.

'No, not yet... I was actually hoping that you would help me with that.'

'What do you mean?' I replied.

'Can you do your power thing so that the hospital says yes when I ask them?' she asked, biting on the inside of her lip.

'I'm sure you're going to be fine; people need to take breaks from pracs all the time.'

'I know but it would just give me peace of mind for when I call... please?' Lana placed her hands in a prayer position in front of her chest.

I laughed at her nervousness. 'Sure, you're going to call whoever you need to speak to at the hospital, ask for a break and he is going to say, *have three weeks off, that's fine, you can come back to the rest of your practical later.* And at the same time, I'm going to call Lisa and she is going to cover for me for the same amount of time.' I jumped out of bed with the phone in my hand. As I stood up, I looked outside of the double doors of the room and noticed Kas was sitting out there sipping a coffee with Matty and Eli. I wasn't sure where the other guys were. I wondered if I also snored next to him last night. 'Okay, I'm going to make the call in the bathroom.'

'I'm going to go for a walk outside,' Lana announced, before trailing down the hallway and out of the villa.

'Amy, do you need to call anyone?' I looked at her making herself at home on Kas's bed.

'No, I just sent a text. If they're not happy with that then they can fire me,' she said with a shrug. 'Cause whatever, *this* is an adventure.' She threw her arms up in the air. 'And I tell you what, Daph, I've got a feeling we're heading towards bigger and better things.'

I grinned. 'I better make this call then.'

Once inside the bathroom, I caught a glimpse of myself in the mirror. My hair was in disarray, and I was still wearing Kas's shirt, draped around my body like a short dress. I set my phone on the counter and splashed my face with water. I pulled a peach-coloured towel off the rack next to the shower and patted my face dry. Once I felt and looked a little fresher, I picked up my phone again and slid onto the cold bathroom floor, leaning my back against the bath.

I looked at my phone for what must have been the first time since dinner the night before. There was a missed call from my mother. She was off holidaying in Greece with her new boyfriend—she could wait. There was also a text message from James sent at 7:00 a.m., it read, *just doing the polite housemate thing and checking you're not dead.* Unless I was staying at Levi's house, it was very rare for me not to come home at night.

I quickly replied, *I'm all good, I'll call you later.* I scrolled through the contacts, found Lisa's number and hit call.

She picked up straight away. 'Good morning beautiful, how are you on this glorious morning?' She chirped through the phone.

I didn't feel like being completely honest about the banging in my head and my churning stomach. Instead, I cleared my throat. 'I'm really good thanks. I had a good sleep, I needed it. I just wanted to give you a quick call and ask a really random favour.'

'Oh, I'm so glad. Sure, hun, anything.'

'I've been thinking about getting out of town, just having a break from here, you know? After everything with Levi, I think I need it. Lana and Amy kind of offered it to me as they both have time off work in the coming weeks. I know it's super late notice, but I just wanted to see...'

Technically I wasn't lying. It felt like the real reason I was going. For the adventure, for something fun, to try out being a groupie for a little while.

'Honestly Daph, I couldn't agree more. This town can get so consuming. Take a couple of weeks off and get out of here. Winter is hitting and it gets quieter in the store now anyway. Don't worry, I'll rearrange the roster and cover you.'

I released a breath I didn't know I was holding. 'You are an absolute godsend, Lis.'

'No, you deserve it. Where are you planning on going?'

'Umm... Melbourne first.'

'Oh yes, you have to go shopping. Noah Still just opened a pop-up store there, try something on for me and tell me what it's like.' Lisa's voice had already changed from compassionate to excited.

'Oh my gosh, I definitely will.'

'Okay, I'm just about to order a coffee lovely, so I'll let you go. It's all good though, just take your time and keep me in the loop.'

'I will, thank you. Chat soon.'

I hung up the phone, stretched my arms out and took a deep breath. I felt the flutters in my heart from last night come flooding back. I took a couple of deep breaths, running my hand through my hair and shaking my head. 'What is happening?' I whispered out loud to myself, thinking about the events of the past 24 hours. I looked down at my phone, scrolling through Instagram and typing in 'Tuned In'. They had one million followers. Geeze, how had I not heard of them before now?

And there she was, a first picture of Casey, close up, speaking into the microphone on stage. Yes. She was tagged. @Casey. McQuinn. I clicked straight onto her profile. A message couldn't hurt right? Maybe Casey would be able to explain what was going on. I ran my eyes over her grid for a couple more seconds before typing her a message.

Hello Casey, you probably don't remember me but my name is Daphne, I was at your most recent seminar in Brisbane and I need to chat to you about something. If you could get back to me ASAP that would be great.

I hit send. My heart fluttered. I wanted to know what was going on, but still a part of me didn't. Amy was right, this was one of the best things that had ever happened in my life. Why should I be questioning it? I didn't want this to end, not right now and not for the next three weeks.

I hoisted myself up from the floor and walked back into the bedroom to meet the girls. As I closed the bathroom door behind me, both Lana and Amy were sitting upright on the edge of the bed, eagerly waiting for the verdict.

'What did he say?' I asked Lana.

Her straight face cracked into a smile. 'He said, "have three weeks off, we can add them back on at the end of the year"!'

'And I've got all the time I need off too!' I shrieked.

'YES!' Amy screamed. The girls leapt off the bed and pull me into a hug. 'This is going to be the best adventure of our lives!' Amy added.

Our lively hug was interrupted by the sound of the balcony door sliding open. 'I'm guessing you ladies got the all-clear,' Matty noted.

We released each other and turned towards Matty, Eli and Kas. I locked eyes with Kas; it was the first time I had seen him all morning. His green eyes looked even more dreamy when they were a little dark and tired. His hair was scruffy and he was clutching his coffee mug like it was his lifeline.

'We're going on tour!' Amy screamed.

'I'll text the other guys and I'll get Issy to grab the car so you can pick up your stuff,' Eli said.

'Do I have time to have a quick shower?' I asked Kas.

'Go for it,' he said.

'I'd really love a coffee too.'

'We'll get you one on the way,' he promised with a smile.

I smiled back at him and turned towards the shower.

Chapter 9

'I need a nap,' Eli said as we all piled into the lobby of the Melbourne hotel. It wasn't quite as dreamy as Sync, but it was fancy and exclusive. Tall ceilings and large chandeliers.

Lana came running back to where we were all sitting. 'Guys, there's a piano bar here. Literally, a bar that is filled with grand pianos. Someone order me a negroni right now!'

I laughed as she took a seat down on the lounge next to me. I was feeling a lot better after a business class nap, a coffee and a Hydrolyte. Plus, the excitement of an adventure in an unfamiliar city did wonders for my hangover. I only had the foggiest of memories of Melbourne from when I visited as a kid.

'I don't want to nap. We all slept on the plane, anyway. I want to make the most out of this trip. Who wants to explore the city and go shopping?' Amy stood up and clapped her hands. She had more energy than all of us put together.

'I do.' I raised my hand and stood up.

'Yep, I'm in too,' Lana said.

'Any other takers?' Amy asked.

Each band member looked half dead. Nolan was cutting laps of the reception area talking to someone on the phone. He never seemed to stop working.

'You go have fun girls,' Issy chimed in. 'I'll make sure all your luggage is organised and we'll see you for our dinner reservation at 6:30 p.m.'

'We will be back for dinner, all shopped out and looking as hot as ever,' Amy said. Eli threw a wink in her direction, Kas smiled, and I think Jack was asleep. The three of us grabbed our handbags, leaving our suitcases in the more than capable hands of Issy.

We strutted out the front door of the hotel together.

'Okay girls, so now we're alone, tell me the goss. What happened last night?' Amy asked.

'Firstly, where are we going?' Lana asked as we walked up the street. 'I don't think we're too far from Colins Street, that's where we need to be.' She grabbed her phone out of her bag to google the distance.

'Yes, let's make a serious plan for this shopping trip. Today we are standing in the middle of Australia's shopping mecca and we can have whatever we want! How much time do we have? Actually, you know what, I think I need a hair of the dog first.' Amy pointed to what looked like a tiny cocktail bar. 'Let's get you that negroni, Lana.' Amy walked faster and crossed the road while Lana and I tagged behind. 'Daphne darling, work your magic, will you?' she smiled back at me.

We're all about to receive free negronis.

'The cute man that I see in the distance behind this cocktail bar will make us a negroni, free of charge.' I smiled as we walked closer to the small brown brick building with large windows. The tall glass door was wide open and the array of alcohol bottles could be seen from across the street. We filed in one by one. It was a grungy, cool-looking bar with a spray-painted wall of a cartoon woman smoking a cigar. Vintage brown leather bar stools lined the bar and in the corner was a matching couch and two chairs. The smell of bourbon filled my nostrils.

'Wow, you girls look like you need a pick me up. Big night?' A young man in a light grey button-up shirt smiled brightly from behind the bar. He had short brown hair and a slight gap between his teeth that suited him well.

'Do we really look that bad?' Amy replied, looking down self-consciously at her long, black dress, denim jacket and white converse sneakers.

The man laughed. 'No, nothing a negroni can't fix.'

'Oh fab, that is exactly what we were after. How did you know?'

'I can match any cocktail to a person—it's my superpower, I guess.' I smirked at the comment. 'Take a seat, ladies.' He pointed over to the large lounge chairs. 'First rounds on me.'

'Wow, that's so kind of you,' Amy replied in her sweetest voice. 'But do you mind if we only have one round? We have a lot of things we have to get done in the...' she looked down at her watch, 'next five hours.'

'Absolutely.' The man flashed a smile back and started measuring out spirits. We all took a seat on the brown leather couch.

'Okay, I'm preparing a list,' Amy said as she grabbed her phone out of her bag. 'Going back to my earlier question, where are we going to go? I'll start... I really want to go to Louis Vuitton—I'd love a bag and a pair of shoes or two.' Amy winked at me.

'Lisa told me that Noah Still has opened a pop-up store here. We have to go,' I insisted.

'Just take me to Burberry. I want everything Burberry,' said Lana.

'Perfect, perfect, perfect. I purposely didn't pack much for this trip so that we can stock up on as many designer outfits as possible. We are going to be the best-looking groupies anyone has ever seen,' Amy declared.

'Is that what we are?' I questioned Amy.

'Honey, I know that you're probably still heartbroken over that surfing loser, but let's get real here! In less than twenty-four hours, you've manifested a trip around Australia and you're sleeping with one of the hottest, most talented singers ever! Fuck

Levi. You are the real MVP here!'

'I'm not sleeping with him,' I corrected in a hushed voice.

Amy reared back in shock. 'What? You didn't sleep with Kas last night?'

'No, I didn't. Why? Did you sleep with Eli?'

'All night. In the bed, in the shower, I woke him up in between sleep, and twice this morning,' Amy bragged. 'He is *incredible*, these chances don't come around a lot, hun, you've got to ride them while you can.'

Lana and I laughed. Sometimes I was in awe of Amy; she was so sexually enlightened. I, on the other hand, hadn't thought about anyone other than Levi. Sleeping with someone else wasn't even on my radar.

I looked over at Lana. 'Did you sleep with Jack?' She giggled and nodded as the man from behind the bar brought over our drinks and sat them down on the glass table in between us.

'There you go ladies, enjoy!' he said politely, acting as though he hadn't overheard Amy's very *loud* declarations a moment ago. We took our first sip together—my god they were strong. But Amy was right, the hair of the dog was making me feel even better.

'I mean you don't need to sleep with him, Daph. You do you, always. I'm just saying if I was you, I wouldn't have been able to contain myself.' Amy slurped loudly on her drink.

'He is super attractive, but I don't know. I just want to have as much fun as we can on this trip and go from there,' I replied quietly, hoping the bartender wasn't eavesdropping.

'I think that's the best plan you've ever had,' said Lana. 'You don't need to rush into anything, you don't need a rebound, even if the best possible rebound was sleeping next to you last night—it doesn't matter.'

'Cheers to that.' I clinked my glass with the girls as we all took another large sip.

'I say that we down this quick-smart and hit the shops,' said Amy.

'Good plan,' I agreed.

Together, we downed the drinks as quickly as possible, thanked the cute guy behind the bar and strolled up the street.

'We're only two streets from Colins,' Lana said as we followed her mapping guidance. 'Okay, what's the plan of attack? How did you specifically get the jumpsuit again?' Lana asked me, sounding just as uncertain as I was about how this power worked. I looked down at my phone. I opened my Instagram app to see if I had heard back from Casey but there were no notifications.

'Just leave it to me,' I advised. 'Go into the store, try on everything that you want. Don't look at the price tag and I will see if I can work my magic. If for some reason, it doesn't work out. I don't know, we'll just all pretend we all forgot our wallets.'

'This is starting to sound a little like stealing,' said Lana.

I deflated, feeling the same way after I replayed my own words. How could we knowingly return to the hotel with thousands of dollars' worth of designer clothes in just a few hours?

'Yes Lana, this is stealing; stealing the Burberry you know you were god damn born to wear but you're a broke student so you can't afford it yet,' Amy said so matter-of-factly. Lana giggled, but still looked unconvinced. 'Besides, it's not stealing when the universe literally gave Daphne a power that grants us everything that we want. If that's not God screaming, *girls, you deserve designer*, then I don't know what is.'

We all laughed, the cocktail had kicked in and we were in fine form. We finally approached the top of Collins Street, our eyes wild as we took in the strip of designer stores we'd only ever dreamed of visiting. Lana was still looking down at her phone. 'Oh, it says that the Noah Still pop-up shop is only one-hundred metres from where we are, just down that side street on the left.'

'You're first up baby girl,' Amy nudged me.

I grinned at her eagerly before making my way towards the store.

We walked towards the pop-up store, feeling a little tipsy and exhilarated. Noah Still was a young European designer in his early thirties and he was on my top ten designers list. I remember the moment when his first collection came out, I was in my last year of fashion school and his crochet European summer tops and swimwear blew me away. Since then, he'd gone global, boasting bold summer prints in eveningwear across all seasons.

We approached the old brick building where a security man stood out the front, looking us up and down. He nodded slightly as we walked through the door and passed the window print that read *Noah Still* in classic black Times New Roman font. I wondered idly what font I would use when I brought out my own label.

'Oh my gosh.' Amy walked over to the bright diamond-shaped silk pieces that doubled as a top and a headscarf. I lost Lana to the headbands and walked over to browse Noah's newest collection. There was a lot of white with light blue snake-skin printed silk and sheer dresses that had patterns in all the right places. Noah was a goddess at making any woman's body look like a classy but seductive silhouette of beauty, I admired that about his work. I held out the long, white sheer dress, a matching two-piece set and a light-coloured snake-skin headscarf. It screamed confidence.

'Oh girl, I don't think I've seen anyone walk into these doors as perfect for that outfit as you. Can I take these to the dressing room for you?' A man wearing tight-fitting black pants and a magenta button-up shirt approached me.

'Really?' I said surprised, my eyes widening as I stared at the two piece. I mean it's a beautiful design, but I don't think I could pull it off.'

I knew my body and what worked for me. I could usually tell straight away if a design was meant for me or not, but this one left me a little stumped. Plus, it was super luxe, I had no idea where I would even wear it.

'Trust me, you have to try it on.' The man looked me up and down to ascertain my size and picked up one of each piece from the new collection, strutting off to the change room. I followed quickly.

'What was your name darling?'

'I'm Daphne.'

'Well Daphne, have fun transforming yourself into an absolute goddess.' He hung the clothes and ushered me inside. 'I'm Craig, just shout out if you need anything.' He winked and pulled the curtain closed behind him.

I stripped off my light skinny jeans and white top, carefully slipped one of the sheer dresses over my head and let it fall over my body. I stared back at myself in the mirror. Wow, maybe Craig was right. The design was incredible, the thick shear material exposed nothing, but told a story of desire, confidence, and femininity. I took the headscarf off the rack and wore it exactly like that, around my head like a bandana to add a sense of individuality and edge.

'Daph are you in there?' Lana called out. I opened the curtain and walked out into the hallway of the changeroom. Both Lana and Amy were sat on the velvet cream couch at the end of the common area. They were holding bags, tops and scarves. Their mouths dropped open as I walked out.

'Girl. You. Have. Never. Looked. Better,' Amy said, staring at me with unabashed awe. 'You must get this!'

'We'll get *all of it* and everything will be completely free,' I said, winking at both the girls and walking back into the changeroom.

I didn't bother trying on the rest of the collection, if it didn't look good on, it looked good enough hanging in my wardrobe. I stood opposite Craig at the counter as he wrapped each piece of our chosen purchases into tissue paper and large white paper bags. There were five large bags between us. He added the final piece to the last bag and walked over to his register.

My heart started to beat faster as he tapped his finger on the screen. I still didn't understand the logistics of how this power worked. As soon as this trip was over, I'd have to find Casey from Tuned In and ask her specifically what the hell was going on. Did this happen to everyone that had attended the seminar? No, surely not. Levi had attended the seminar before, and I was almost certain he didn't have that power. 'You girls are going to look like such queens!' Craig said as he continued to tap away.

'Thanks,' I said, smiling shyly. Amy and Lana stood back from the counter behind me.

'Okay, that comes to zero dollars,' Craig said easily. I watched him as the words fell out of his mouth, his eyes twitched, and his voice strained. It was like a glitch. As though for a second, my power had hold of him and he was completely unaware of what he was doing. He typed three zeros in the EFTPOS machine and turned it towards me so I could tap my card. *Beep.* The machine chimed and printed out a receipt to the value of nothing. 'Enjoy Ladies,' Craig said, handing us the bags.

'Thank you so much,' we all replied in almost perfect unison and walked out of the store.

Standing back on Collins Street, we all stared at each other, beaming as we held our new treasured items.

'Right, it's Burberry time, bitch.' Amy smiled and winked at Lana as we strutted down the other end of the street.

Chapter 10

'Hello, we um, we actually don't know what room we're in—
we're here with The Koras,' Amy said, splashing her signature
smile across the hotel reception desk.

'Ladies, I've been waiting for you.' I turned around to hear
Issy's familiar voice as she approached us. 'Don't worry, I have
all your keys. We're all on level ten and your room number is
written on each key.'

'You are the most organised person I know,' Amy marvelled as
Issy handed out our keys.

She smiled sincerely. 'I try.'

'Seriously, you're an angel, I'm considering getting you to join
me back home and help me take care of my life.'

Issy laughed again. 'You're too kind, I'm really glad you're here.
I think it's going to make this tour a lot, um, nicer and light-
hearted to have your energy around,' said Issy. I could see the
cogs already turning in Amy's mind, but Issy quickly continued,
'So dinner is in half an hour. Is that enough time to freshen up
and meet us on the top level.'

'That's perfect timing. We'll see you then,' said Lana.

Issy nodded and walked away. We waddled towards the
elevator; arms filled with shopping bags.

'The boys are going to think that we're rich, walking back in
with all these bags,' Lana said as we stepped into the elevator.

'No, we'll just pretend that Daphne's a much bigger stylist than she says she is and has all the hook-ups in Melbourne. It's a win-win. It increases Daphne's status, and no one will question us about how we got all this stuff,' said Amy.

Lana and I nodded in agreement as the elevator doors opened into level ten. I looked down at my key. 'I'm 1016.'

'I'm 1017,' said Lana

'And I'm 1018.'

'What? I thought we would all be bunking in the same room?' I said, brow furrowed. Last night was fine, Kas was lovely, but I was here to have a fun time with the girls. Not end up in the bed of someone else, while I still nursed a broken heart.

'Yeah... I thought that too,' said Lana.

'Oh, sorry I made it very clear to Issy that when she booked, I would be staying with Eli, so I guess she booked you both in the same situation... so enjoy! You can thank me later,' she said strutting up the hall. 'Let's meet back here just before dinner,' she said, before disappearing through door 1018.

I awkwardly swiped my key against the 1016 door while trying to open it and keep a hold of all my bags. Pressing my weight against the door, I ungracefully fell in. Kas was sitting upright on the bed with his headphones on his ears. He sat up and laughed as he took off his headphones.

He looked down at my arms filled with shopping bags. 'Are you okay?'

'I'm fine. Sorry, I didn't know if you would be here or not,' I said.

'Yeah, I'm just relaxing before dinner. You look like you had a fun day. Do you need help with those bags?' He sat up as though he was coming to help me. His hair was spiked in his trademark style, and his fringe was shaped around his face. He was wearing light denim skinny jeans that were ripped at the knee and an oversized black t-shirt with a green symbol in the middle. I couldn't quite make out what the symbol was, but the green was still bright enough to bring out his eyes.

'I'm fine. Thank you, though.'

The room was huge and it smelled of his cologne, musky yet sweet. I placed my bags down next to where Issy had put my suitcase against the wall with a large, flat-screen TV. A small mini fridge laid underneath a bench in the corner that was equipped with a sink and kettle. One wall of the room was made entirely of glass, exposing an expansive view of the city.

'It's a cool view, hey?' Kas said as though he could hear my thoughts, or maybe he was just reading the awe in my face.

'It's gorgeous.'

'Wait 'til you see the views from dinner tonight. It's going to be so great.' He smiled, checking out the view from the comfort of the large bed. I don't think I had ever seen a bed so big in my life. I could get lost in there.

'Oh yes, dinner. I have to get ready.'

I walked back over to my bags; I already knew the exact items that I wanted to pair together for the night. I selected a pair of Louis heels with my flared Rolla jeans and the Noah Still headscarf, only this time I would wear it as a top.

Kas pointed to the closed door to the left of him. 'The bathroom's through there,' he said as he placed his earphones back in.

◆ ◆ ◆

When I re-emerged from the bathroom sometime later with fresh makeup and my new outfit, Kas stared at me, 'Wow, you look incredible,' he said, his tone soft. He stood by the bar fridge sipping a beer.

'Thank you,' I said with a smile. Craig was right, I did feel like a queen and I was ready to have a fun night. *Take it a little slower on the drinking and don't fall asleep this time,* I chastised myself. I rummaged through my shopping bags in search of my phone.

'Oh, we should get going.' I looked up at Kas when I checked the time.

'Yeah, we should. Are you ready?'

'I am.'

He held out his hand, waiting for me to take his. 'Let's go, lovely lady.' He seemed relaxed but I could see the glimmer of excitement in his eyes.

'Are you excited to play tonight?' I asked as we walked out into the hallway.

'Absolutely, I think I'm always excited to play. Our tours are the best part. It's where you really get the full reaction from everything you have spent months working on in the studio.' He held my hand tight as he sipped his beer in the other. I smiled back at him as we walked towards the elevator. Amy, Lana and Nolan were all standing there. 'Where are the rest of the lads?' Kas asked as we approached them.

'They are already up there,' Amy replied as she tapped on the elevator button. 'Daph, you look amazing,' she said as she looked at me. I noticed her eyes drift down to mine and Kas's interlocked hands.

'Right back at you.' Amy was wearing a peach-coloured silk top with long, white pants, while Lana wore a short black dress with her new checked Burberry heels, her long brown hair hanging past her shoulders in luscious waves.

The elevator doors opened, and we all hopped in.

'What time do we need to be at the venue?' Kas asked Nolan, letting go of my hand as the elevator took us to the top of the building.

'Eight or so—just a short dinner. Just pre-warning, Eli's already had too many,' Nolan said, meeting Kas's eyes. Kas bit his lip and nodded.

The doors of the elevator opened; we stepped out onto what looked like the roof of the building. Dark navy tiles were below our feet and greenery surrounded the edges of the open rectangular roof. A large, long table was dressed with plates and cutlery in the middle of the roof and to the left was a waiter dressed in all white standing behind a makeshift bar. Matty, Eli and Jack were sitting apart from each other but chatting across the table.

The whole roof offered 360-degree views of the city. The sun had almost set, and the lights of buildings shined through the fading sky. As we walked closer towards the table, I spotted an infinity pool, glistening behind the white seats.

'Oh my gosh, we have to go for a swim in the morning!' said Lana.

'Absolutely!' I replied.

'Oh, you've decided to join us,' Matty said, smiling as we all took our seats at the table. Kas and Lana sat on either side of me. Amy sat directly opposite me next to Eli. I turned around as I heard the elevator doors open again and saw Issy emerge. She walked over and waved when she caught me staring at her.

'We've just done the same thing with food again,' Jack said. 'There's just going to be a range of everything. We always find it easier like that before a gig.'

'Sounds perfect,' I said.

The young waiter approached the table as Issy sat down. 'Can I get anyone another drink?' he asked. I noticed there were already a few empty glasses on the table.

'I'll take another,' said Eli raising his glass, slurring his words slightly. His glass was a dark golden, he must have been drinking bourbon or whisky.

'I'll grab a beer,' said Kas.

'I'd just love a vodka soda,' I chimed in, deciding on the cleanest alcoholic beverage I could think of.

'Oh, that's a smart idea,' said Lana. 'Make that two.'

'Actually, make it three.' Amy smiled back at the waiter.

'Perfect. Anything else?' Everyone shook their heads, he headed back to the bar.

'So, what did everyone get up to today?' Amy asked, being a gracious dinner guest in the middle of the table, looking towards Eli.

'I napped and then had a couple of drinks,' Eli said as he turned back to Amy. I saw Amy sitting a little taller in her seat, leaning further away from him with each word as if she could smell a distillery oozing from his breath. 'You look fucking delicious.'

He licked his lips and moved his left hand around to the back of Amy's neck, pulling her towards him in a kiss. She jerked at this, but he pulled her fiercely and met her lips in an open-mouthed kiss. Kas touched my knee under the table. I turned to look at him and his wide, open eyes met mine. He squeezed my knee tighter as if to say something. Maybe it was a warning. It seemed that Eli liked to drink, maybe he was trying to tell me he had it under control. After a few seconds, Amy pulled away politely smiling. Eli seemed to think he was whispering in her ear but the whole table could hear him when he said, 'I love that outfit, but I'm going to love it more later when it's on my floor.' Amy usually loved this banter, but this time he was too drunk and his words seemed less fun. She just threw him a cheeky wink and then turned back towards the table, her smile dropped, and I watched her gulp down. She met my eyes; I nodded my head towards the elevator doors but she shook her head and looked away.

'I think all of us just had a good old nap,' Jack said, smiling. 'But you girls do look like you had an epic day.'

'I haven't been to Melbourne in so long. It's so great to be here,' said Lana.

'I think Melbourne is glad that you're here. Well, I'm glad you're here,' said Jack.

The waiter came over and placed our drinks down in front of

us. At the same time, two young waitresses appeared with three plates each, placed them in the middle of the table and quickly scurried off.

Today's cuisine looked like a mix of healthy Mediterranean and thank god because I was in need of some nutrients. Plates were filled with lamb chops and tzatziki dip, prawns, felafels, sweet potato chips, spanakopita, and olives. One of the waiters reappeared with two large bowls, one with stir-fried vegetables and the other, a large Greek salad.

We all hurriedly filled our plates, as though we hadn't eaten in days. It was delicious. Eli was the first to break the silence when he called out to the waiter for another drink. Unlike the rest of the table, his plate was full. He had to go on stage tonight— surely, he'd eat something.

Kas wriggled in his set, sitting up taller and setting down his cutlery. He rested his elbows on the table and rested his chin on his fists. 'Eli, mate, come on. We've got to be on stage in a couple of hours.' Kas's tone was light, but his eyes told a different story.

The look Eli flashed Kas in return was so intense, I felt my heart jump a little. 'Exactly, mate,' Eli snapped. 'We're not on stage for another two hours, so I can have exactly two more drinks.' His eyes made my stomach squirm. I took another bite of lamb to try and settle it.

'Eli.' Nolan stood up from the table, speaking sternly, as though he was a principal talking down to a child in trouble. He turned and addressed the waiter, 'No more drinks thanks mate, we're good. We're good for the whole table, in fact.' The waiter walked away as swiftly as he walked over.

'Speak for yourself,' Amy muttered lightly underneath her breath, taking a sip of her drink. It looked like I was the only one who had heard her speak.

'Righto Nolan, kill the party for everyone why don't you?' Eli snarled back.

'I'm not killing the party for anyone, I'm saving it. You've got to play at the party tonight and I don't think all the people who bought tickets to see you tonight want to see a sloppy drunk guy on stage.'

Eli cackled, leaning back in his seat. 'A sloppy drunk guy? Really that's all you got?'

'I could say a lot worse, and you know it, but if you haven't realised, we're actually in the company of some lovely respectable women.'

'Ha, respectable… you should see her behind closed doors.' Eli wrapped his arm around Amy but she quickly swiped it away. Eli sat up in his seat, beading his eyes at her but she didn't flinch.

'Amy I'm so sorry, you can be excused,' Nolan said, expecting Amy to leave the table.

'I know that, and no it's fine. I'm going to finish my dinner thanks.' Amy reached out to the trays of food, placing some more eggplant on her plate, pretending as though nothing was happing next to her, while the tension across the rest of the table rose.

Eli's demon eyes glanced around the table. 'Does anyone else have anything that they want to add to this conversation or can I hurry and order another fucking drink.'

'You're not ordering a drink,' Kas said, leaning back in his seat, sipping on his.

'Do you think I'm a sloppy drunk guy as well?' Eli said, mimicking Nolan.

'Yeah, I do. And I know I wouldn't be the only one in this room that agrees with that. But honestly, I don't care if you want to drink your life away, go for it. As your friend I wish you wouldn't, as your friend I think it's time you grew out of it, we all have. It's not the fucking rockstar way anymore. It's time to move on. But as your band mate, it sucks even more when you're drunk. You think you're fine, but you're not, you're all over the stage and we're constantly having to pick up your slack.' Kas kept his eyes on Eli, and I watched Eli's grow darker with every word.

'Do you agree? Do you all agree with that?' Eli aggressively pointed around the table, but no one spoke up, staring back at him emotionless.

'Jack, you're my older brother, are you going to have my back here?' he screamed louder pointing directly at Jack.

'Let's just cut the drinks for tonight,' said Jack softly, holding tight onto Lana's hand.

Eli cackled again but didn't speak up, he pouted his lips and nodded, squinting a death stare onto each one of us. My spine shivered, I looked up at Amy but she seemed completely unshaken, staring down at her plate, chewing away on some more lamb.

'I'll be downstairs.' Nolan glared tiredly, then stormed off for the elevator.

I looked around the table as everyone dropped their heads, chewing their food in silence. I glanced wide-eyed at Amy and mouthed, *are you okay?* She flashed a warm smile and took another sip from her drink.

Kas nudged me lightly, whispering, 'Are you okay there?'

I smiled back at him. 'Yeah, I'm fine.'

'After Melbourne, we're heading to Sydney,' he said, leaning in towards me, quickly changing the conversation. 'My sister lives close to where we usually stay there, we could organise a dinner together with the lovely Ms Meyers, I'm sure she would love to meet you.'

My heart skipped a beat. 'Really?' I asked, barely containing a squeal. My thoughts from the drama that just unfolded disappeared, and my mind flashed back to the conversation with Amy in the bathroom from the night before. *This could be an incredible opportunity for you. This could launch the next stage of your career.*

'Yeah absolutely, I feel as though you two should meet, you would get along so well. I'll give my sister a call after dinner and get her to organise something,' he said.

'Wow. This is incredible. Thank you. Like really, thank you.'

I wanted to jump for freaking joy. I took another sip of my vodka soda and turned back towards the room. Everyone was back to engaging in small conversations with each other, as though the blow up with Eli was nothing out of the ordinary. Plates were empty and bellies full. Amy and Eli were kissing. She pulled away, staring into his eyes and he was smiling back at her. Maybe a bit of food had calmed him down. I looked over at Lana, both of us glared back at Eli and Amy. My stomach churned watching them kiss, why did she have to be into him? He was such a dick. What was she doing? She was better than him and this. I had to get her away from him. But selfishly I couldn't stop my heart from flipping. I felt as though I knew exactly why I was here. I knew exactly why I had been given this gift. It was for who I was about to meet, the career leaps and bounds that this could lead to. This was exactly where I needed to be. Fuck Levi. I was about to manifest a life beyond being a small-town surfer's wife. I was about to finally make my biggest break in the fashion world. One beyond my wildest dreams. But no, I couldn't. Not with what was happening right in front of me. I shook my head out of my daydream. Pulling my phone out of my bag, I looked down at it in my lap. Shit. Still nothing from Casey.

Jack jumped up, looking at his phone. 'Nolan just messaged me. He's downstairs and wants us to leave for the venue in ten. We should probably head back to our rooms before we go.'

Everyone followed Jack's lead, standing up from the table and heading towards the elevator. I stood behind my chair, taking a deep breath staring out into the night lights of the city. I readjusted my top and smiled. Kas held his hand out in front of me and I interlocked my fingers with his.

'Are you ready?' he said.

'Born ready... just um, I'll meet you down there. I just need to visit the bathroom...' I grabbed onto Amy's hand, and she followed me back towards the restaurant bathrooms. Lana caught the drift and scurried quickly behind.

I closed the bathroom door behind us and spun around towards Amy. 'Are you okay?' I said, leaning in close and cornering her.

'Yeah, why?' She stared back at Lana and I wide-eyed, trying to look as though we didn't know what we were questioning her about.

'Seriously? Is he a psycho? Do we need to leave now, because we can?' Lana said.

'Eli is fine, he just I guess, sometimes drinks a little too much. But what do you expect,' she shrugged her shoulders, 'he's a rockstar?'

'We can all get Issy to move us into the same room? Heck, if we need to leave, I'm sure she could book us a flight,' I said.

'And cut this adventure early? Are you kidding me? So what Eli had a little bit too much to drink, I'm fine, he's fine, we're all fine and we're all going to go and have one hell of a night. You girls need to stop overreacting.' Her voice got louder, and she threw her arms out.

'We just care, that's all,' said Lana, 'and this doesn't seem like a once off to me.'

'Look you guys know me, and you should know I don't put up with bullshit or anything that I can't completely handle. So can we please just move past the shit bloke that he is tonight and not let that ruin our fun. Let's be honest, we're all here for ourselves at the end of the day anyway. So, what if Eli's a dick on alcohol, I'll have a chat to him about it when he's sober and we can all continue on,' said Amy.

'I don't know. I don't like the guy,' said Lana, stamping her foot down, leaning into one hip.

'I second that,' I said, crossing my arms in front of my chest.

Amy sighed, leaning against the wall. 'I just want to have fun girls; can we please just go back to having fun. If he's out of line again. You don't have anything to worry about, I will put him in his place that's for sure! But can we just stop and look around at where we are right now. Let's not let a guy get in the way of this!' We stood in silence. Amy's eyes pleaded with us to drop it. Lana's shoulders finally dropped and I uncrossed my arms.

'Okay, but if I see any shittier behaviour from him. It is most definitely not going to be just you that Eli is going to have to answer too,' I said.

Amy nodded. 'I know, and I know you have the power. You can make anything happen to him,' she said, shrugging. I bit the inside of my bottom lip. I had never thought of that before, what I said and what I thought was becoming reality. Which meant I could possibly manifest really bad things too. I really needed to watch my thoughts.

'Okay, now can we go back out there and have a good time now?' Amy asked. She stood up straight, checking herself out in the bathroom mirror.

'Guys, we're going to Sydney soon, and Kas is going to introduce me to Sophia Meyers.'

'No way, what?' Lana screamed, covering her mouth with her hands, staring back at me wide eyed, hoping her scream didn't echo outside of the bathroom.

I laughed. 'Yeah.'

'See girl! This is huge, this is the start of something so big, we're not going to finish this adventure now, are you kidding me?' said Amy.

I was so excited; I could feel tears of happiness start to well in my eyes.

'Let's go out there and make more magic happen!' Amy said,

walking past me, opening the door. Lana and I stood still smiling at each other.

Amy popped her head back into the bathroom. 'But um… Daph, I'm going to need you, because well, you're the magic one in this situation right here.'

I laughed. 'Coming.'

Chapter 11

'Are you excited?' Sitting in the back of the SUV, Kas squeezed my shoulder.

'I just...' I paused, taking a deep breath. 'I just can't believe that I'm here.'

We'd landed in Sydney a few hours ago. This was the first night that I was staying away from the girls and the rest of the band. The last couple of nights in Melbourne had been a blast. The shows were incredible. I was enjoying watching Kas in his element, he was born for the stage, and it exuded out of him. If you met him on the street, you wouldn't be aware of his talent. He was quiet, almost shy, but when he was under lights with a microphone in hand, it was as though something else ignited in him. It was beautiful. I guess it was the same as when I got to dress someone, or when I would doodle designs during a quiet day at work. Which reminded me, I had to call Lisa and check in to see how the store was going. But I'd do it after tonight, I couldn't wait to tell her about how I had met the real Lady Meyers. I wondered how I could frame the story without telling her about my power. I wanted to keep this between Lana, Amy and myself—I didn't need anyone else to know how weird I'd become.

'What do you mean?' Kas leaned in closer, placing his hand on my knee. It felt different sitting in a back seat of a nice car with him as a paid stranger drove us around. The past couple of days had felt surreal but the most amazing, perfect kind of surreal, as though my life had just become a movie.

'I guess if someone told me last week that I would be sitting in a back of a car with the lead singer of The Koras on the way to have dinner with Sophia Meyers, I definitely would have laughed in their face.'

Kas studied me with his perfect green eyes. He seemed to do this a lot. I wondered what he was thinking. It often seemed like he was analysing me or trying to read me in a certain way. Since we'd left for Melbourne, I wasn't really sure what to think of us. We'd flirted, held hands, and had been sleeping beside each other for a couple of nights. But we never cuddled, let alone kissed.

'You intrigue me, Daphne,' he said.

'How so?'

'You come across so confident. You have this spark, this energy, this attitude in the way that you are and the way that you dress. But then sometimes you speak, and I guess, it makes me question it. Like maybe you don't truly believe in your power or what you're capable of.'

My body tensed and I looked away. I felt exposed, as though I was just caught out in public, naked and exposed with no make-up. Fuck. This guy could read me well.

'Sorry, honestly. It's none of my business. I didn't mean to intrude.' Kas took his hand off my knee and sat further back into his seat.

'No... it's okay. I guess I'm just not really used to having such open, honest conversations—not with men at least. I'm not used to someone who hardly knows me, understanding me so well.' I gulped down and turned away, my body still stiff.

'Yeah,' he laughed. 'Sorry it's just, you do intrigue me.' He laughed again, watching my expression. 'Sorry, I'll stop, I'll stop.'

I took a deep breath and sank deeper into the cushioned

leather car seat. My body had started to relax but I was still nervous. What would Sophia Meyers think of me? I was wearing her jumpsuit. It was the only time in my life I'd been unsure of what to wear. Kas reassured me that it was a good idea, that it would be flattering, not weird, to rock up to dinner in the designer's clothes. I guess I would have loved that if I had my own collection.

Sophia Meyers will love you and will want to work with you.

I looked back towards Kas. His head was now buried in his phone. 'But... what do you mean when you say... my power?' I asked shyly.

Kas looked up from his phone and smiled. 'A lot more is possible than you let yourself believe.' I wished I could tell him how much that was becoming apparent to me right then and there. I looked back out the window. Kas's phone light went out as he placed it back into his pocket. 'Did anyone else mention what they were getting up to tonight?' he asked.

'Amy, Lana, Jack and Eli were all going to catch a movie together, have some dinner and then grab a massage back at the hotel,' I said. 'Nolan said he had a lot of work to do, and I don't know what Matty and Issy were getting up to.'

'Cute, double date. What is going on with those guys?' Kas looked at me like I knew all the answers, but I just shrugged. 'Oh, come on. I know women talk about everything.'

'Well, I think the chemistry between Amy and Eli is pretty obvious.'

'Hmmm... I wonder how long it will take for that fire to burn out,' Kas pondered. I was thinking the exact same thing. They were intense, their time together was heated—emotionally and physically. Right now, they were ablaze, but we all had eyes on them, waiting for something to burn a little too hot. 'I don't know if Eli will ever calm down.' I agreed with Kas's remark. I hadn't known Eli for long, but he was an intense person. He loved attention, he loved to be the centre of the crowd, he loved fame and he also loved to drink. If anything, he would have made a great front man. 'What about Lana and Jack though? They seem kind of sweet together.'

I smiled at Kas's comment. 'They do seem really sweet together. It's super cute. I don't know, though, she's keeping pretty quiet. I think she might be a little bit smitten. I guess she isn't wanting to say much because she doesn't want to get too carried away. This whole experience is a bit out of the ordinary I guess... it doesn't seem like real life.' I paused realising what I'd said. 'I don't mean that in a bad way, I know this is your real life—it's an amazing life—it's just... Lana doesn't know if it fits into her life.'

'Yeah, I understand that. That's the hardest thing about always being on the road,' Kas replied. 'I guess this is a strange situation, to have three girls with us. Three amazing girls. Sorry, not girls, women. It's just not the norm. It is really great though,' Kas said.

I smiled back and butted in, 'Yeah, Amy thinks that we're strange...'

'Us? As in me and you?'

'Yeah. Amy thinks that it's really strange that we're not sleeping together,' I blurted out.

'Is this your polite way of asking me into bed with you?' Kas winked at me and then laughed.

'I've been in your bed Kas,' I replied confidently, half-flirting. 'More than once, in fact,' I laughed. 'But no, I umm... I don't think it's weird. Actually, sleeping next to someone I hardly know is a little strange.'

'I think inviting someone I hardly know to come and join you on your tour is a little strange. It's not a bad thing. But I'm also a firm believer that everything happens for a reason. Everything that is meant to be, will be.'

'I don't think we can really say *hardly know* anymore. I think you can read me pretty well.' My voice was almost a whisper. He smiled but stayed silent. The car came to a stop.

The grey-haired man behind the steering wheel, dressed in a black suit, turned around to Kas. 'What time would you like me to pick you up?'

'Can I text you like twenty minutes before we're ready to leave?'

'Done,' the man replied. Kas jumped out of the car so quick and had already run around to my side of the door and opened it for me before I could even unbuckle my seatbelt.

'Why thank you,' I said, looking up at him standing tall, holding the car door open. He was wearing a dark grey button-up shirt with his black ripped skinny jeans and a white pair of dress shoes. As my eyes travelled up to his face, I smiled. His hair spiked in his usual way. I really liked his style; effortless in the way few people could pull off without trying.

'Are you ready, milady?' he said. I smiled wider, flashing my teeth. Kas's words reminded me of James. I should message him and make sure that everything back home was okay.

He smiled, holding his now familiar hand out for me. I took hold of it, hopping out of the car, and he closed the door behind me. A tall grey apartment building with a large gate awaited us. I followed Kas's lead as we walked towards the keypad and intercom to the right-hand side of the gate. He pushed the apartment number and rang the dial button. The intercom only chimed twice before a clear cheery voice rang through the phone. 'Is that my long-lost brother?' the friendly voice spoke with excitement.

'Hey Ruby,' Kas said, leaning into the speaker.

'And did you bring this lovely girl with you?' she said again, still sounding excited and comically suspicious. It suddenly dawned on me that I was about to meet some of Kas's family. I'd never even met any of Levi's family before.

'I have. Daphne's right here next to me.'

'Eeek,' Ruby squealed through the phone and the gate slid open. It opened to some greenery and a couple of car spaces. To the right looked like the opening of an underground car park for residents. Ruby had buzzed the door leading into the apartment complex open, and we walked straight on through to a large, open lobby with four elevators. Kas pressed the button for the next elevator.

'My sister is lovely. She can just be a little full on sometimes, maybe over enthusiastic. But I'm sure you'll get along fine.'

I smiled, glancing down at our interlocked hands. What was I doing here holding his hand about to meet his family?

'Sophia will probably already be here too,' he said.

We rode three levels up to apartment 32. Just as Kas went to knock on the door it flew wide open. I let go of his hand. A gorgeous, brightly smiling woman opened the door—Ruby. I wasn't too sure how old Ruby was, but Kas had referred to her as his older sister. She looked to be in her mid-thirties, but it was hard to tell. Her brunette curls bounced as she threw her arms open and brought Kas into a long hug. She wore a long, pale yellow strappy dress that hugged her petite body perfectly. She finally let go of Kas's embrace and turned towards me, she had the same sparkling green eyes as Kas, plainly giving away that they were siblings.

'And you must be Daphne.' She grinned, holding out her arms and embracing me in a hug. 'It's so nice to meet you. Kas never brings girls home. Come on in.'

I smiled back at her and shot a glance at Kas. Did she think that we were together? Did I have to go along with it to get Sophia Meyers's approval? Kas glanced back at me and shrugged. He held his hand out, gesturing for me to walk through the door first. I went to slip my clear heels off, when Ruby turned around. 'Oh hun, your outfit is divine, please keep the shoes on.'

I grinned. 'Wow, I feel so understood,' I admitted. Ruby

flashed a smile back at me knowing exactly what I meant. I followed Kas closely behind. The hallway opened to Ruby's large white open kitchen. It was beautiful, boasting a large marble island bench with three pendant globes dangling above. There were several other downlights scattered throughout the space, creating different focal points within the room. It was the kind of kitchen that made even the most amateur of cooks like me envious. A tall lean man with olive skin and a large smile was pottering away over the stove.

'This is the lovely chef, Steve,' Ruby said.

'Hello,' Steve spoke shyly, before turning back to attend to his pots and pans.

'Hey Steve,' Kas and I replied almost in unison.

'Steve is seriously amazing. Jeff and I have just been so busy lately, we've hired him for a couple of dinner parties, and we honestly wish he was here every night,' Ruby said as she walked up to the sliding doors behind the kitchen and opened them up, exposing a large deck with an outdoor marble dining table that took up most of the space. Driving here in the dark, I didn't realise how close it was to the river. Her house had a stunning view of the Harbour.

'Kas and Daphne are here, guys,' Ruby said as she walked out towards the table. A man at least ten years older than Ruby stood up from behind the round table and threw a friendly arm around Kas.

'It's so good to see you, mate. It's been a long time. We've missed you!'

Kas patted the man's back. 'Yeah, it feels good to be back.'

'And welcome Daphne, I'm Jeff.' Jeff placed one arm around me and kissed my cheek.

'Lovely to meet you, Jeff.'

'Likewise,' he said, making me wonder again what Jeff and Ruby had heard about me from Kas before this dinner. 'Just make yourself at home here, alright,' he said kindly. 'I'll get us all a glass of wine.'

'Daphne, you look like an absolute dream!' A tall, lean woman with a blonde pixie cut and wearing a light blue silk dress walked towards me. She moved so gracefully in the short distance between the door and where I was standing that it felt like the balcony had transformed into her very own catwalk. I'd watched dozens of her interviews over the years, but she looked even more striking in person.

'Please, please would you give me a spin.' She held her hands in a prayer position in front of her chest and I smiled back at her. Gracefully, I took a slow spin, nervously trying to remember my steps from primary school ballet classes. 'Ah, you were right Kas, you were right. My god, you've got a good eye boy!' Sophia leaned in to hug Kas.

'Good to see you, Soph.'

'Right back at you.'

I couldn't help but interrupt their intimate moment. 'A good eye?'

'Yes, darling. Kas told me that he had met the woman who was the vision for my new collection, and he was completely right. You are exactly what I imagined. Did you get anything else?' she asked.

I blushed. Here I was standing in front of my favourite Australian designer—I wanted to say yes but I couldn't lie. My bank account could hardly support the entire new Lady Meyers collection. I also couldn't tell her that I'd received her best piece for free. 'No,' I replied softly. 'I just have the jumpsuit.'

'Darling, Daphne. Let me hook you up with the rest. I have to give you the rest, it was made for you, I swear.'

'A glass of Pinot anyone?' Jeff reappeared carrying a silver tray filled with five wine glasses and a bottle of red.

'Yes please,' Ruby chimed in, pulling a chair out from the table.

'Come and have a seat, dinner shouldn't be too far away.'

I walked over to the table and pulled up a seat between Kas and Sophia, while Ruby sat across from me. Jeff filled our glasses.

'So, Daphne, Kas said that you're a stylist?' Sophia took a sip from her wine and sank back in her chair.

'Yes,' Ruby chimed in. 'Tell us everything Daphne, I want to know more about you.' My insides squirmed with both nerves and excitement. Sophia Meyers was sitting next to me and the sister of a bloody rockstar wanted to know about my small-town styling career. Maybe I should have thanked Levi, rather than be angry at him; Tuned In really did change my life. Although, I did feel a little out of place. I wanted to slowly shrink from the table, knowing that I didn't completely belong at this table when it came to the success of my creative career. *You've got this. Think of your power, you've made it this far. Anything can come of this. You can get the career opportunity of your lifetime.*

I sat a little taller in my seat. 'Yes, I am a stylist at a small store in Byon Bay.'

'Oh, how lovely. I do need to visit my store there more often, it's a fabulous getaway. Well, you certainly have amazing taste Daphne, you're obviously in the right career. They must be lucky to have you.'

I blushed again at Sophia's words; she was lovelier in person than I could have ever imagined. 'Thank you, honestly Sophia, I'd be lying if I didn't say your designs have had a huge impact on my career.' For a minute, I was surprised by my surge of confidence.

'Thank you, Daphne, that's really beautiful of you to say. I think to be an inspiration of some sort is something that many people strive for in creative careers. You'd have to agree with me, wouldn't you Kas?'

Kas nodded while sipping his wine.

'The entree is ready.'

Steve appeared holding three plates. He sat them down in front of Kas, Sophia and myself, before disappearing and returning with two more plates for Ruby and Jeff.

'Entrée is scallop ceviche with a prawn dumpling,' he said and then quickly disappeared back into the kitchen again. I loved Asian-infused cuisine—it looked amazing. Jeff, Ruby and Kas started to pick apart their entrée, eating it in small tasteful bites.

As I picked up my knife and fork, Sophia blurted, 'Let me dress you.'

She hadn't touched her meal, instead, she leaned further back in her chair and observed me carefully over her glass of wine.

'For what?' I asked, trying not to let my imagination run wild.

'Surely you're going to the Arias?' Sophia said.

'Oh, I hadn't told Daphne about them yet,' Kas jumped in.

'What do you mean you haven't told her, they're next week!' Sophia sat back up in her chair, furrowing her brow at Kas.

'My typical brother, always last-minute,' said Ruby with a roll of her eyes.

I cut into my ceviche and ate a piece of the delicious scallop as the rest of the table bickered.

'I'm sorry Daphne.' Kas turned towards me. 'Would you like to go to the Arias with me?'

I looked back into his green eyes, trying to read his expression. 'I would love to come with you,' I said, thrilled.

Sophia clapped excitedly. 'Perfect, I have to dress you Daphne— you have to let me dress you.'

'Of course. I would love that.' I smiled back at her before taking another bite of my entrée, trying to act like this exact moment was normal and my heart wasn't beating a thousand miles per hour, ready to leap out of my chest.

'Perfect. I already have a vision. I'm going to get started on this tomorrow. I'll get my team to call you and book in a fitting.' Sophia swirled her wine then finally tucked into her food.

'Kas, what are you and the rest of the guys wearing? Will they be bringing along dates as well?'

I was Kas's date. I could have pinched myself right there under the table.

'I haven't even thought about it yet, Nolan is probably organising it for us. But yeah, no doubt Eli and Jack will be bringing their ladies.'

'So, you'll all be on the red carpet in a group?' Sophia asked Kas as her eyes wandered between the two of us.

'Yeah,' Kas said as he placed his cutlery on his empty plate.

'Hmm....' Sophia muttered as she chewed. She swallowed and continued, 'I'm not going to have time to dress three women... Daphne, why don't you?' Sophia asked.

'Why don't I dress my friends for the Arias?'

'Yes, dress the whole band too. It would be wonderful exposure for you. Aren't you guys nominated for a couple of awards?' Sophia stared at Kas intently and he nodded. 'Perfect, they'll win, no doubt,' she said confidently. 'They will be pictured everywhere. It would be a fantastic opportunity for you career-wise.'

My head was spinning. I wanted to jump for joy, stand up on the gorgeous marble table and scream, *hell yes*, but I had no personal relationships with any designers—they were all run through Duskk. I just dressed people in the clothes that we already ordered in the store. I looked back at Sophia. She was staring at me intently, waiting for my answer. I didn't have the contacts for designers, but I did know how to make that happen.

The most amazing designers are going to want to work with me.

'I'd love to dress them,' I replied. 'Sounds amazing.'

'Fantastic. I really want my design to take the lead though. I'll show you what I've put together after tomorrow and we will come up with a full concept for the whole crew.'

I set my cutlery on my empty plate, grinning from ear to ear. 'It's a pleasure doing business together, Sophia.'

She laughed. 'Oh, you're just divine Daphne, this is going to be great.'

Steve reappeared from behind me, reaching in between Kas and me as he collected both of our plates. 'More wine?' he asked the table.

'That would be lovely, thank you,' Jeff replied before staring directly at us both. 'Tell us, how exactly did you meet?'

'Oh yes, please tell us,' Ruby said. 'I was so shocked when I got a call from Kas telling me that he was bringing someone to dinner.'

I took a deep breath and downed my final sip of wine. That must have been all Kas said, which finally calmed my nerves. Ruby had just jumped to the conclusion that we must be together. I still had no idea how to answer their question as everyone leaned in waiting for us to expose some sort of beautiful love story to them. My cheeks turned red again and I looked towards Kas, hoping he would take control of the situation.

'We met before a gig at a restaurant. Daphne and I started talking and I invited her to come along to the show, I guess we've been inseparable ever since.' Kas looked towards me, placing his hand on top of mine. He flashed me a wink and smiled.

'Aw how lovely,' Ruby doted. Steve returned, making his way around the table and refilling our glasses. 'So, Daphne, how is it being on the road with the boys? Are you able to work on the road as well?'

'I've taken a break for now, but I will need to head back to the store soon,' I said to Ruby.

'Just wait darling, you may never have to go back to the store. Not after next week, everyone from every city will want to be working with you. You could pick and choose your work wherever the boys have to play,' said Sophia.

My heart skipped a beat, I didn't know if I could handle any more of this, I'd end up in hospital with heart failure. Not only was Kas's own family trying to make sure that our fictional relationship would last, but I was reminded that Levi's family never even knew I existed. They lived in Brisbane and anytime he would visit them, he would make the trip alone. Here I was two weeks later sitting with Kas, his sister, and her best friend as they helped me build my career—and I'd met them less than an hour ago. *Don't get too ahead of yourself. It's happening because you created it, you're only here right now because of your power.*

I stared at Sophia blankly. 'Do you really think that would happen? I mean, this is just one event.'

'We're creatives. Fashion, music, art, whatever. We create, which means we create the reality of what can be true. Sounds like you might have been playing it small for too long lovely.'

I smiled back at her. If only she knew how much I was creating my life right now. But maybe she was right, maybe I had been thinking too small. Maybe that's how I had been living my whole life.

'How is 5:00 p.m. on Monday for a fitting? Kas knows where our studio is,' said Sophia, checking her phone calendar.

'Two days from now?'

'Yes, is that okay with you?' She glanced up towards me.

'Yes, I was just making sure that it was enough time for you?' I replied softly.

'More than enough,' she answered. 'Just like I said, us creatives, we can make anything happen.'

Chapter 12

'I wonder what she is going to dress you in,' Lana said. She was sitting on the floor of Kas's hotel room, leaning against the bed and biting down on an apple.

Amy sat up from the bed and slowly walked over to the small table in the corner of the room that was filled with fruit, cheese and crackers. She picked up a couple of grapes. 'Yeah, I want to know too. I mean, you know her style, have you got any idea?'

'Well, if it's a custom piece I'm guessing it will be something that will tie in with the new collection so that people see it and want to buy it.' I stood in front of the full-length mirror on the door of the closet, fixing my lip gloss.

'You're literally going to be an overnight model. People all over the world are going to see your photos and want to buy Lady Meyers. This is crazy,' Lana marvelled.

'Um... all of us are going to be. In fact, what you're both going to wear is what is more important to me.' I turned back towards the girls. Amy sat back on the bed.

'Yes. I'm excited to see our outfits! And to be on the red carpet! I was born for this. My day has truly come. Daphne, you need to nail this so that we all look amazing. I never want to go home, let's just live in hotels for the rest of our lives. Maybe one of us should have a baby... I'll do it,' Amy blurted out, having a direct conversation with the rambling thoughts in her head.

Lana almost choked on her apple. 'You would have a baby? With Eli?'

Amy shrugged. 'He is pretty great.' Lana narrowed her eyes on Amy. I hadn't seen Eli since the last incident, but I knew Lana was keeping a close eye on the two of them.

'Yeah?' I asked, curious. 'I haven't asked how things are going with you two...'

'He is *so* fun.' She smiled but said nothing further.

'I guess I just never spoke to you after dinner the other night in Melbourne,' I prodded.

'Yeah, he got a little too drunk. He said sorry, he also wanted me to apologise to you girls for it as well. Sometimes he said his drinking can get a little out of hand when he is stressed on the road with so many shows and little sleep, but he promised it wouldn't happen again.'

Amy stood up and returned to the platter of food, brushing off my question.

'So, you would have a baby with him?' I sat still, staring at her. I knew she was smitten with the loser, but I didn't know how much.

'Well, why not? Let's be honest Daph, he is an absolute catch.' Amy picked up a cracker and some cheese, chewing as she continued talking. 'Like, he does have his life together, you know. He is successful and attractive and fun and carefree. I can't say I've met any man back home like this before. So, hell yeah, I would have his baby. But obviously right now, I'm joking...' She paused, swallowing the last of the biscuit. 'But what about you and Kas, you literally met his family!' Amy said, changing the conversation back on to me.

'Yeah, talk about moving fast Daph. Meeting the fam before you've even hooked up,' Lana jumped in, laughing. 'What were they like?'

'I just met his sister and her partner. They were lovely. And Kas and I are just friends—he was doing me a favour.'

'An unbelievable favour. Honestly, what a sweetheart to

organise a dinner like that,' Amy said as the front door to the hotel room opened, silencing our conversation. We all turned in unison to see Kas walking through the door looking ever so casual with his messy hair and black clothes. He hadn't styled it today—I kind of liked it like that. Amy was right. It was nice, it was incredibly nice. But how was I to know if it was real? Or if it happened just because I thought it, just because of how badly I wanted it.

'And here he is,' Amy said with a knowing smile. 'We were just speaking about you, angel.'

'Angel?' Kas flashed Amy a puzzled smile.

'Oh, we just were saying how lovely it was that you organised a dinner for Daph to meet Sophia.'

'Oh, it's nothing. I know Soph well. She was probably more excited to meet Daphne. I knew she'd want to work with her.' Kas plopped a grape in his mouth and turned towards me. 'Speaking of, we should get going and see what she's got in store for you.'

I leapt off the bed excitedly and grabbed my handbag from the bedside table. 'I'll be back ladies.'

'Have fun and don't forget to take a million and one pictures. You'll need them for when you're styling us,' said Amy.

◆ ◆ ◆

Once we were in the back seat of the car, Kas said, 'I've got to head to the radio station and do a couple of voice recordings and promo stuff. It's only around the corner from Sophia's studio, so I'll get Dave to drop you off and then you can message me when you're done. I reckon we'll be finished at the same time.'

'Perfect.'

'Are you excited?'

I was sitting to the left of him with my legs close together and my hands intertwined in mylap, I must have looked like I was posing for a school photo. I laughed, took a deep breath and relaxed into the car seat. 'I'm a little nervous.'

Kas laughed. 'Really? I couldn't tell.'

'Here we are,' Dave called out from the front seat as the car stopped. I looked out the window and there it was. A tiny doorway on one of Sydney's main streets that boasted Lady Meyers famous name in her bold black and white italicised signage above the door.

Kas reached out and placed his hand on top of mine. 'You have nothing to be nervous about. It's going to be great,' he reassured me.

I took another deep breath and nodded before opening the car door and hopping out of the car. 'I'll call you when I'm done.'

'Have fun.' He smiled and I closed the car door.

I couldn't believe I was here, standing directly in front of the Lady Meyers flagship designer studio. I had dreamed of this one day. Maybe when I was older and had my own significant event to go to. But I never imagined that it would come so soon. Thank god for my power.

I opened the glass door and closed it gently behind me, hoping I didn't make too much of a sound. The doorway opened straight up to a set of shiny timber stairs with fresh white walls on either side. I'd taken three steps up when—'Daphne! I'm so glad you're here. Your timing couldn't have been better. I'm ready for you.' I looked up and Sophia was standing at the top of the stairs with her arms wide open. I smiled back at her and quickened my steps to meet her embrace.

'I can't believe you have created something so quickly. I can't wait to see it!' I said as she dropped her arms.

'I can't wait to see it on you, I think it is my best yet. You must come.' Sophia walked in front of me, weaving down a hall that opened to a large designing room filled with mannequins, tables of materials, and pieces from all of Sophia's previous collections, which hung along the back of the room. Beneath my feet was the most divine shaggy off-white carpet. It felt wrong to wear shoes inside, I wanted to feel it in between my toes. To the left of me stood a wall of mirrors. Two men stood around a mannequin that was draped in white.

'Daphne, meet my two favourite men and main designers, Heath and Colin.'

'Oh, you are so beautiful,' Heath said, approaching me and studying my frame carefully. He wasn't being rude, but it still made me nervous to have someone observe me so intently. I stood stiffly and gulped, feeling a little out of my comfort zone. 'I can't wait to see you in the gown. It's going to be perfect for you.'

'I told you. Time to strip down Daphne, I have to put this on you,' said Sophia.

Colin stepped back from the mannequin and for the first time, I saw the white silhouette in all its glory. If my body was stiff before, it was now frozen. My jaw dropped open. Sophia smiled wider as she watched my response. 'It's gorgeous, isn't it?'

She was right, it was the best design from Sophia Meyers I had ever seen, and it was an original made for me. I couldn't fathom it. Sophia and her designers had eloquently dressed the mannequin in sheer white material that flowed out from the hips. I imagined how it would bounce around me like a sexy Cinderella gown along the red carpet. The top of the dress had a sheer, white-boned corset designed to create a stunning hourglass figure. I imagined myself standing next to Kas dressed in a slick black tux. We'd look perfect. The dress was an absolute statement piece, and I could already envision how I could dress Amy and Lana alongside me.

'Well, are you going to just stand there with your mouth open or do I finally get to see it on you?'

I managed to finally close my mouth and give a shaky nod. I kicked my boots off, and as I took off my jacket off Colin held out his arm for support. I slipped my dress off and passed it to Colin, while Heath and Sophia unbuttoned the corset from the mannequin. Heath lifted the half-plastic body out of the way, exposing its silver leg. I stepped inside the middle of the dress as Heath and Sophia pulled the corset up over my body, holding it tight together and clipping the back closed. I breathed deeply and squeezed my chest into the material until I felt the last clasp close. Sophia, Colin and Heath backed up their steps and we all stood in front of the mirror, admiring the gown.

It was the most fabulous I'd ever felt in my whole life.

'Are you ready to steal the fucking show my darling?' Sophia's lips curled up. She stared intensely into the mirror, looking at me as though she was Cruella Devil and she'd just spotted a dalmatian.

'Look at it. Look at her. This dress is going to be in glamour magazines across the freaking globe,' said Sophia. 'This year, there's no god damn doubt we're getting invited to Milan. You might as well pack your bags now boys.' Sophia took one last look at me in the mirror and her smile turned into a stiff poker face. 'Okay, take it off. I can't have it getting ruined.' Sophia clicked her fingers at the men standing around me and started walking towards the back of the room. 'Daphne, meet me in my office once you're dressed, I just have a couple of things I want to go over with you regarding the night, your styling etc.' She threw her arms up in the air in excitement, flashed me a quick smile and exited the room.

I let a breath out, staring at myself in the mirror. I was wearing a custom Lady Meyers. It seemed like yesterday I was denying myself a second coffee for the day because it was stretching my budget. *That was last week.*

'How do you feel?' Colin said to me underneath his breath.

'Honestly, I... I'm speechless.'

'I think this really is her best piece yet, and I've been a part of all her designs,' said Heath.

'Yeah, I... I'm overwhelmed by it all.' I was living a life beyond my wildest dreams. My confidence started to sink with my shoulders, I didn't know if I really deserved all this.

'I think it's even better that you're a nobody too, it's going to be a viral 21st century Cinderella moment... I think this might even make you bigger than Machine Gun Kelly and Megan Fox. Daphne and Kas, the new it couple. Better enjoy the next week girl, cause soon enough, everyone is going to want to know about you.' Heath's smile widened as he clapped his hands in rhythm with his giggles, already excited by the future gossip articles.

I took a deep gulp, feeling a rock come up in my throat. If I was completely honest, I hadn't thought about that. I hadn't thought about 'being known'? Accolades for my career sure, but even what I wanted to achieve was always kept hidden away between my pursed lips, spoken loudly to only a few. I hadn't thought about having my personal life on display. Because the truth was, it was all a lie. Kas and I weren't even together. And now we were about to deceive the world, for what? My career? This was his career too...why was he going to all this effort for me? Why did he even care? None of this was real. None of it made sense. And I still had no idea what this power was and where it came from. My head started to spin, and I felt my stomach churn and the temperature rise up my body. I went to take a deep breath, but my eyes started to drift towards the ceiling.

'Daphne!' Colin screamed in my ear as I felt four hands on my back.

'Oh girl, don't starve yourself, you're much better than that,' said Heath as he and Colin helped me back up from my short fall. I blinked a couple of times starting to gain a back a clear view of the room. 'The dress fits perfectly, in fact, don't go losing any weight.' Heath started to unbutton the corset, as Colin and I held it in place.

'Sorry, you're right. I probably just need a nutritious meal.' As the boys pulled the dress down, I took a step out of it, walking over to my bag and clothes in the corner of the room, quickly redressing myself and reaching for my phone in my bag. It was 4:00 p.m. I guess I'd only had two eggs and a slice of toast this morning, and a few crackers with the girls this afternoon. I did need to eat. But I also knew that wasn't why I fell.

'Here.' Colin tapped on my shoulder. I turned around to him passing me a large glass of water.

'Thank you,' I said, before quickly guzzling it down. 'So which way is Sophia's office?'

'Up the hall, second door to the left, you'll see her name on the door.'

'Thanks.'

Chapter 13

'Drink Daphne?' Sophia stood in the corner of her large office pouring herself a drink from the champagne bottle sitting on her marble bench that matched her large marble desk. I sat in one of the white velvet office chairs and admired her light grey wall blanketed in awards.

'Oh, I'm okay. Thank you.' I'd woken up this morning, after way too many nights of drinking, promising myself that I would say no to alcohol anywhere I could. Drinks that expanded outside of Friday and Saturday night were never a thing for me, not even in fashion school, and my body was starting to notice it.

'Are you sure? This is a celebration.' She turned around towards me, throwing her glass up in the air and taking a sip from it.

'Sorry, I'm still feeling the effects from too much red wine last night,' I politely declined again.

'Oh, don't tell me you're not much of a drinker? You're on tour with Kas's band. Don't those men drink like fish?'

I laughed nervously, hoping that I didn't have to decline the one and only Sophia Meyers again. 'Oh no, there's another gig tonight. I'm sure there will be a lot more drinking again,' I lied. I knew full well I was going to ask Kas if he would mind if I skipped out on the gig for an early night.

'Oh lovely, I really should get to one of his shows while they are in town.' She sat down on her grey velvet chair behind her desk, staring at the large computer screen.

'So, Daphne, I just wanted to run a couple of the rules I have put in place for when it comes to styling the band members and their friends.'

'Rules?'

Sophia sat back in her seat and laughed. 'Not rules. Um. Suggestions, I guess.' She smiled but her eyes stared coldly towards me. 'It's just that a dress like the one I have just designed, I need it partnered with the right pieces, as I am sure you are aware, and I have absolutely no doubt that you'll create the wonderful overall look.' She sat up in her chair and leaned in closer, placing her elbows on the desk. Her eyes met mine and I wondered how long she could hold a gaze without blinking. She sure as hell could do it longer than me. 'Just don't forget you're the star of the show... and my dress is the centerpiece.'

'Oh absolutely, I understand that.'

'Great,' said Sophia, slamming a piece of paper down on the desk in front of me. 'This is the list of stylists I have compiled for you. They will work wonderfully with the dress, some of them are local and some of them will send you pieces... now I haven't had a chance to get in contact with them about the event, but I trust that you'll be able to organise something amazing with them?'

My eyes scanned through the list. There were only six names and contact numbers. I recognised three local designers, and three names I had never heard of before.

'You don't have to use all of them, just whoever you think is right for the job... I trust you, okay.'

'You can trust me; I am going to make your dress shine so bright. I can't thank you enough for this opportunity.'

'No thank you Daphne, you're rare you know. I can see it in your eyes how much you can see my vision. I'm glad you're in the industry.'

'Knock knock.' I turned around to see Kas closing the office door behind him.

'Kas.' Sophia got up from her seat to great him with a warm hug.

'Sorry, I finished early, so I thought I would pop over... maybe catch a glimpse of the dress?' Kas asked hopefully as he brushed his hand along my shoulder and took a seat down next to me.

'No, no, no, you can't see it till awards night. Don't worry though, I've given Daphne a list of all the best designers I know to get you looking ever so sexy next to her.' I felt my spine tingle. It was Kas's award night at the end of the day not mine. 'You guys are going to make a much bigger statement than last year.'

'What happened last year?' I asked.

'They all chucked black blazers over their usual stage gear. It was appalling.'

Kas laughed and a cheeky smile spread across his face.

'Anyway, Kas can I offer you a drink?' said Sophia, taking another sip of hers.

'Oh, I'm okay. If you ladies are done, we should really be getting back for dinner. It's an earlier stage call tonight.'

'Of course, the show beckons.'

'I'd probably get started on that list tomorrow, Daphne; we haven't got many days left.'

'Tomorrow? I'll be getting started on it tonight,' I reassured Sophia, picking up the paper off her spotless desk and following Kas's lead as he opened the office door for me.

Chapter 14

'Did you get a picture of the dress? I need to see it; I need to see what I'm working with,' Amy said, as the three of us power-walked along the river.

'It's so freaking dumb that I didn't. Absolute rookie error, but don't worry I have a very clear picture of it in my mind. I did a deep google of the designers Sophia recommended I work with last night. Let's take a seat in here, I'll show you.' I pointed to a little coffee shop with outdoor seating up ahead, providing us with full views of Sydney Harbour.

'Good morning, ladies, just coffee or are you after something to eat as well.' The young waiter with a Dutch accent approached us before we could all sit down at the rectangular alfresco table.

'I could eat.'

'Yeah, I think we'll do breakfast,' said Lana.

'I'll bring over some menus,' the waiter said before scurrying away.

'Is this a free breakfast?' Amy asked, looking at me.

I rolled my eyes. 'Yes, this is a free breakfast, we will not have to pay for this breakfast.' I took a deep breath as I sat down. I don't know why I'd rolled my eyes; I don't know why I was starting to get sick of this power. I shouldn't be. It had gotten me to this very moment. It felt crazy how much life had changed in the past week, yet how quickly I'd embodied it, like it was normal.

'Okay, here is what I'm thinking.' I handed my phone to Amy, my photo album open on the two screenshotted dresses

I had shortlisted from the last night. 'The first one would be you Amy and the second Lana.' Lana wiggled her seat a little closer, craning her neck so she could ger a glimpse of the photo. They both stared emotionless at the phone. 'I haven't decided on shoes, accessories, etc. yet.'

'You want to dress me in white?' Amy scrunched her face up. 'I mean style wise, classic; I absolutely get it... but if this is the first time I am going to be seen by a potential global audience, I don't really think that white screams "AMY".'

'But Amy, this isn't your award show, it's the boys,' Lana replied as she took the phone out of Amy's hand, staring closer into the white dress that I'd also chosen for her.

'Yes, but boy's fashion is boring. Dress any man up in a suit, who is usually wearing a band T-shirt, and everyone is going to love it. We're the ones that get to dress-up their style, duh. The Arias are just like the Brownlows, no one watches the red carpet for the blokes.'

'Yeah... you do have a point. I think I've already decided on each of the suits. Kas is going to be in a long jacket and a bow tie.'

'Oh, I do like that idea,' Lana said, handing me back my phone. She inclined her head quizzically at me. 'Did you get any sleep last night?'

'That was the plan, but I couldn't help myself. Besides I need these pieces express posted like right now, I have five days and that includes today!'

After we'd left Sophia's, I joined everyone for dinner but missed the show, I needed an early night in. It was true, I did. The bags under my eyes where bigger than the Louis we bought days before.

'I did get more sleep than you guys though. I didn't even hear Kas come in last night, what time was it?'

'I couldn't tell you, he wasn't drinking though, he left earlier than all of us.'

'Daphne, I know you know what you're doing. I know that this is your thing. But, classic? I just don't get it. You're the queen of bringing everyone's natural essence out in their style. I wouldn't call any of us... classic?' Amy frowned.

'Can I get you ladies a coffee to start?' The waitress came back over, placing a fancy clipboard menu in front of each of us.

'Latte,' Amy said quickly, looking straight back at me.

'I'll have an almond milk cappuccino,' said Lana.

'Make that two and large.' I smiled back at the waitress as she nodded and walked away. Lana looked down at the breakfast menu, but Amy didn't take her eyes off me. I knew she was right.

'I know... it's just... the designers that Sophia gave me to work with only really create straight paneled, neutral stuff. And it goes with the theme of the dress that Sophia made, I guess.'

Lana lifted her head out of the menu. 'When you first put on the dress, what did you envision? What did you see for the whole group?'

'You were in sparkling red, and Amy a seaweed green.' Amy's eyes lit up as I spoke. 'It was ballsy, it clashed. But in between the white ball gown and the slim lined suits. It screamed electric elegance. Which in some way, is how I see this whole situation, The Koras, us, the music industry, the very fact we're here right now.'

'Was it a Noah Still seaweed green?' Amy asked, intrigued.

'It was.'

The waitress reappeared with our coffees.

'Wow that was quick,' I said as she placed a large cup with a perfect chocolate swirl in front of me.

'Yeah, you ladies have come at the right time, you've missed the morning rush before work. Are you ready to order?'

'Yes,' Lana quickly jumped in, as Amy and I scanned the menu.

'Can I please have the Breakfast Bowl and add extra bacon?'

'I'll just grab the eggs on toast,' said Amy.

'I'll have the Chia Pudding.'

'Thank you,' the waiter replied as we each handed her our menus. 'They won't be long.'

'Well, I don't know about you Lana, but I vote for option two,' Amy said as she picked up her latte, sinking deeper into her seat.

'I do love red,' said Lana.

'Well, that's all well and good, but how on earth do I get in contact with Noah?'

Amy rolled her eyes at me, just the same as I did to her moments before. I dipped my teaspoon into my coffee, tasting the sweet chocolatey froth, giggling with the spoon in my mouth. Oh, I did have an on again off again relationship with this power. Right now, it was my sweetest lover in the peak of our honeymoon period and things where just about to hit next level.

Noah Still will help me dress Amy and Lana.

'I'll google a stockiest.' I picked up my phone. 'Oh, there's a pop-up store in Sydney too!'

'Perfect!' said Amy.

'But what about Sophia? She specifically told me to only work with these designers.'

'Probably because she doesn't trust you yet. No offence, but she hardly knows you. Neutrals were easy to work with,' said Lana.

'Yeah, I wouldn't stress, she will be speechless once she sees the looks you can really create,' said Amy.

Chapter 15

'So, what's the plan?' Lana looked at me as we all stood side by side in the middle Sydney's CBD, staring emotionless into the glass windows of Noah Still's pop-up store.

'Noah Still wants to work with me, dressing Lana and Amy in my exact vision for the Aria's,' I said calmly.

'Is that it?' Lana stared at me blankly.

'What do you mean is that it? That's all I've been doing all this time. Don't freak me out.'

'Sorry.'

We all took a deep breath in unison and took steps towards the door.

Loud dreamy music echoed off the four walls of the store. It was larger than Melbourne's. Noah's newest season designs were on display, but older classic pieces had my eyes gleaming towards the back of the room.

'Morning ladies, are you looking for anything in particular?' I turned towards the tall dark male standing a meter away from us. My eyes quickly dropped towards his name badge, it read 'Usher' as in, the singer, I thought and then stood up taller, matching his eyes with a smile.

'Hello Usher, I'm Daphne Holmes, nice to meet you,' I said, holding my hand out to shake his.

He stood still, looking dumb founded by the fact that I knew his name, until his eyes dropped down to his name badge, and he chuckled, taking a while for him to catch on.

'Hello Daphne Holmes, pleasure to meet you,' he said as he shook my hand. 'How can I help you today.'

'I'm a stylist and I am dressing a couple of people for the Arias next week. Well, I'm dressing The Koras actually and their girlfriends. These are their girlfriends.' I pointed towards Amy and Lana as each of them stood either side of me.

'Lovely to meet you too...' Usher said as he held his hand out towards Amy and then to Lana.

'Hi, I'm Amy.'

'I'm Lana.'

'Pleasure, ladies.'

'Anyway, as I'm sure you are aware, the Arias are a pretty big deal for Australia and...'

'Oh, you don't have to tell me twice, I can hook you up with a Zoom meeting with his team straight away. I'm not just an assistant here, I know Noah well. I travel around the world for Noah, building, marketing, and running his pop-up stores. Noah has just started his Australian take-over, he is still in Italy, but he is hoping to come and spend some time down here in the coming months.' Usher waved us over behind the counter as he tapped away at the computer screen. 'This is actually an amazing opportunity for Noah, so thank you Daphne I have no doubt he will jump on board.' Usher looked down at his watch and then stared back at me. 'What's your email address?'

'Oh, um, it's Daphne dot Holmes at Gmail dot com.'

'Perfect. I'm just sending Noah's assistant an email now. It's 7:00 p.m. in Italy but she is pretty good at replying quickly. No doubt she will be in touch in the morning, well, our tonight, to set up a meeting. Is that okay?' Usher looked up from the computer screen.

'Yes, that's perfect. Thank you so much, you're extremely helpful,' I said.

'No worries, I'm excited to see you wonderful ladies dressed up in Noah, you're going to glow on that red carpet,' he said with excitement in his eyes, as though it was already a done deal.

'Thank you,' Amy gleamed. 'We're very excited too.'

'Is there anything else I can help you guys out with today? Do you want to have a look at the newest collection?'

'We already bought it in the Melbourne pop-up store. Noah has become one of my faves,' said Lana. Any designer talk was usually well and truly out of Lana's usual vocabulary. She was becoming easily influenced by our new lavish life.

'He's an absolute genius, isn't he,' Usher agreed.

'He is a visionary,' Lana said in now what seemed to be some type of accent, but I wasn't too sure what or who she was trying to channel.

I giggled. 'Thank you, Usher, you've been a dream. But we've got a lot more we've got to get to.'

'Oh of course ladies, thanks for stopping by, I'll be making sure that I tune into the Arias' red carpet.'

I nodded and smiled as the three of us walked back out the glass doors. Walking down the mall, I couldn't help but break out into laughter. Excited and overwhelmed by everything that was happening, I stood still and took a deep breathe. Amy and Lana stopped and swung back around. I looked up towards the top of the buildings and spun around, taking in the essence of the city and bright blue sky above. I looked back at the girls as they stood still, wondering what on earth I was doing.

'I'm not scared anymore. I'm owning this. This power was given to me for a reason. I'm still bewildered as to what that reason is, but I'm here for it. I'm embracing it and if this is the beginning, I'm so excited for what's to come.' I'd given up on waiting for Casey to reply. By this stage I had just come to terms with the fact that she was never going to. This was my new life. I'd been given a power, an absolute gift to make absolutely anything that I wanted to happen. So, without fear, that was exactly what I was going to do.

'Girl, I had no idea that you were even scared about this,' said Amy, gluing her concerned eyes on me.

'I don't know, it made me feel a little uncertain. Like I'd robbed someone else of the opportunity to have this power. Like why me? There's so many more people who could have been given this, who deserve it a hell of a lot more than I do.'

'Do you think other people have it too? Like everyone that has been to that seminar?' said Lana.

Amy laughed almost spitting out her coffee. 'Surely not. Levi's been to that seminar, if he had this power, I would have hoped the loser would have done a little bit more with his life.'

'I don't know. I messaged the presenter on Instagram, but I never got a reply. I don't know how else to get answers. And Amy's right, there's no way Levi would have this or know about this. I'm almost certain. I'd love to know more; I'd love answers to know what's going on with me. But when I stop and look around, well look at where we are. This is magic, and there's no one else in the world I would rather be doing this with.'

The girls smiled and walked towards me, and we embraced each other in a three-way hug. 'You're right Daph, I don't think we should question it,' said Lana, as we let go of our embrace and continued to walk back down the street in the direction of our hotel. 'And who knows where this is going to take us next!'

'Well, I say, we should have a drink and celebrate our fabulousness,' Amy said, strutting down the street. She really was the perfect candidate for red carpet spotlight.

Lana looked down at her watch. 'Amy it's eleven twenty, we're all wearing activewear and we've hardly slept.'

'What do you suggest that we do today then?'

'The world is our oyster,' I said as we reached the traffic lights. I looked down at my phone in my hand as I heard it buzz. I clicked into my email notification.

Dear Daphne,
Lovely to E-Meet you!
I have just received Usher's email and I told Noah straight away,
he can't wait to chat to you more about what you have in mind.
Are you free in two hours' time? I'll send you though an invite
to a Zoom meeting with him.
Let me know if this works.
Regards,
Angelia Zo
Executive Assistant to Noah Still

'Oh my god. We are not going for a drink. I have to get back to the hotel now, I have a meeting with Noah Still in two hours!'

Chapter 16

'You look puffed, did you go for a run?' Kas looked at me as I burst open the front door, accidently slamming it behind me.

'I guess you could say that' I said breathless. I wasn't much of a runner; Amy and I had followed behind Lana as we ran home as quickly as we could.

I was showered and ready to look the best I possibly could on a screen. I threw my bag on the bed and paced up and down the room, thinking about what I should wear.

'Hey, what's going on? Are you okay?'

'Yeahhh...' I stopped and smiled at Kas, who was sitting up on the furthest side of the bed, reading a book. The cover looked fantasy, maybe sci-fi like.

'Are you sure?' He put the book down on the side-table and wiggled over to sit up straight on the edge of the bed.

'Yeah, I'm amazing, I mean, I've never been better.' My voice strained and my eyes welled. I was usually so good at holding them back, gulping down the lump in my throat, but this time they started to flow down my face, I wasn't even sure why they were there. 'I'm great. I really am, I promise. I just...' I sat down on the edge of the bed next to Kas as the tears started to flow heavier. He threw his arms around me, hugging my head tight into his chest. 'I don't know.'

'Hey, it's okay.' His voice vibrated through his chest. Soft like my favourite song. I finally caught enough breaths to stop weeping into his shirt, sit up and unlock myself from his embrace.

Kas looked at me, tucking my hair behind my ear as I sat staring at the blank wall in front of me, which had a piece of ghastly hotel room flower art. Kas moved his hand from my ear to the middle of my back rubbing it softly.

'I'm sorry, I don't even have time for tears. I have to get ready.' I went to get up from the bed, but Kas gently pulled me back down.

'Hey, hey, hey, you don't get away from this that quick, what's going on? What do you need to get ready for?' he asked softly. I could feel his eyes on me, but I couldn't look towards him, I kept my eyes glued on the flower painting. I hated people seeing me cry.

'I have a Zoom meeting with Noah Still, he's a really large Italian designer, he's going to help me dress the girls,' I finally blurted out.

'That's amazing Daph! You don't have to be scared about that...'

'I'm not scared. I'm happy, extremely happy, these are happy tears I promise.' I finally built up the courage to look at him. I caught his eyes and smiled, but my eyes continued to weep.

'Are you sure they're happy tears?' he asked, wiping a tear away from my cheek.

'They are, I promise. I guess I'm just... I'm just overwhelmed. A lot has happened in the past couple of weeks and all of it is so amazing and overwhelming and incredible and a lot. I just have a lot of emotions right now. And you've been a part of this, thank you for inviting me here and introducing me to Sophia,' I said.

'Technically, I didn't invite you. I think our friends just really wanted to hook up.'

I laughed. 'You're right.' Technically it wasn't even because of that. It was because of whatever Casey or Tuned In gifted me with. Which was nagging at the back of my mind, without this power, would Kas even want me here?

'And I introduced you to Sophia because I knew straight from the bat that she would love you. You looked incredible in her jumpsuit, you're an absolute dream for her to dress and I can see the light in your eyes when you talk about fashion. That look, is my favourite look in anyone, it's how I look when I'm playing or creating music. I haven't seen much of that look outside of myself lately and it's been really refreshing to be around. So maybe I need to thank you.'

'I know what you're talking about. I guess in my lifetime I've only seen that look in a few people too.' My tears finally stopped, I took a deep breath and wiped my face. 'But still, it must have been a lot, to introduce me, to lie to your sister that I was your girlfriend. It's like overnight you've become this really important person in my life, and I'm not even sure how it happened.'

Kas's eyes stayed on mine, neither of us blinked. All I saw was the deep lines in his eyes and the slow rise and fall of his chest. 'I didn't mean to involve you in a lie, but for the record... you're not hard to lie about.'

I didn't know what to say, I think I'd stopped breathing. Mouth slightly open, my airways got caught halfway through my exhale as his hand once again reached in to tuck my hair that had unleashed behind my ear.

I didn't leave his gaze. I leaned in, my eyes closed, and felt his soft lips on mine as his left hand held my cheek and placed his right on my knee. Moving in rhythm just as I'd imagined, once, or twice, as I watched him sing every night.

I pulled away, looking down, and bit my bottom lip. Kas, with his hand still on my cheek, lifted my chin resting his forehead on mine.

'Thank you,' he whispered.

'For what?'

'For giving me the chance to get to know you... for being here.'

I smiled. 'I really have to get ready,' I whispered back.

'I know, go have a shower... do you need me to set up a comfortable desk space for you?'

'Sure,' I replied as I pulled my head away from his. Catching his eye briefly, I smiled before running over to the bathroom.

◆ ◆ ◆

'You look amazing. Is there anything else you need?' Kas asked as he stood by the room's door. I felt fresh from a warm shower, a light coat of make-up, a quick blow dry, a comfortable pair of jeans and one of Noah's large head scarfs I was now wearing as a wrap top.

'Honestly this is perfect, I can't thank you enough,' I said, sitting at my new makeshift office. Kas had sourced an ergonomic office chair from one of the boardrooms in the hotel and paired it with the table in the corner of the room, which we usually used for snacks, and set up his laptop for me. I hadn't even thought of bringing mine, I guess I wasn't thinking about much when getting ready for this trip. If there was anything I needed, I could just ask for it.

'Okay, I'm just going to pop over to Jack's and see if he wants to go grab some lunch out somewhere. Good luck, not that you need it.'

'Thank you.'

Kas ducked his head back into the room as his body hung halfway out the door. 'Message me once you're done if you would like to meet us or just grab yourself something from room service.'

'I'll message you.' I smiled back to him as Kas closed the door shut behind him.

I took a deep breath and wiggled around in my chair, sitting up tall. I stared back at the screen in front of me, I clicked on the Zoom link in my emails. My heart skipped a beat. I took another deep breath, squinting my eyes shut, gulping down.

You've got this Daph, I thought, opening my eyes and clicking on the square to join.

I waited patiently for a couple of minutes before the fabulous Noah Still himself appeared on the screen and my face lit up seeing his.

'Daphne!' he said with excitement, exposing his perfectly white teeth. They were too perfect, they must have been veneers. 'I've heard wonderful things, well actually I only just heard about you a moment ago, but I believe you have a very special project you would like me to get involved in.' His square face perfectly trimmed brown beard and luscious curly brown locks shined through my screen. He seemed a little too excited by my 'proposal'. I guess I hadn't thought about how the opportunity would help him, maybe I'd talked up the Arias a little too much.

'Yes, I'm dressing two lovely girls for the Arias. They are the girlfriends of The Koras, a popular Australian band that has been nominated for most of the awards on the night. I'll be standing with them, as I am also dating the lead singer,' I spoke confidently through my smile. 'I've already organised what the boys will be wearing, and Sophia Meyers has organised a custom piece for me...'

'Sophia Meyers? As in *the* Lady Meyers? Oh, I love her work, she is iconic.'

'Yeah, she's really great.'

'I'm planning to come to Australia soon, you must introduce us.'

'Oh yes, I'd love to for sure,' I replied a little shocked, feeling at though Noah and I were now on a friend's basis.

'I'm in by the way, I should have already said that at the start. What are you envisioning for the other girls? How many girls did you say there are again?'

'Two. I would love to see Amy in your signature seaweed green and for Lana, I think she needs something extra shiny, sparkles, red. I know it sounds ballsy and the colors clash. But the men will be in sleek suits with a slight edge of grunge style: thin ties, bow ties, one tux jacket, and my dress is classic white. The overall vision needs to suit the band, be edgy, different, showcase the incredible musos they are... in amazing style of course.'

Noah nodded and pursed his lips. Even though we were half a world away, speaking through a screen, I could see it in his eyes, the look. The creation he was seeing appear in front of it. 'I understand you; I see it, I see the whole thing. Do you trust me to leave this with me? I believe we're on a serious time crunch.'

'I'm hoping to have the dresses in the next three days,' I said nervously. 'And yes, I 100% trust you, this is why I came to you. I love your work.'

'Done. They will be shipped express tomorrow afternoon, whatever time that is for you. Email through their dimensions and I'll whip something up first thing in the morning. Oh, and I love the scarf, I'll be sure to send you some samples of the next collection you'll love them!'

'Whip something up?'

'Yes. I've got the seaweed green piece you're talking about but the red sparkles, oh that's something out of my comfort zone... please send me some shots of the girls, I'd love to really envision their complexions with the pieces.'

'Done, done and done. I'll get those to you in the next half an hour.'

'Perfect, pleasure doing business with you Daphne, what a treasure I've met! I haven't made any talented Australian stylist friends yet, so this is wonderful. Get me to Australia ASAP.'

'No, thank you. I am very excited to work together.' I matched his smile.

'Now I'm so sorry, I've got to run lovely; I have an event to go to, but I will chat to you very soon.'

The Zoom call ended, and I closed the screen of Kas's laptop. I picked up my phone and sent Kas a quick message.

Sorry I won't be joining you for lunch. I've got some more work to get done here. I'll grab some room service soon. See you later x

Chapter 17

It was the morning of the Aria's.

'Breakfast in bed?' Kas whispered in my ear as we lay snuggled in white sheets. The sun had been beaming through the crack in the blinds for hours now, it would have to have been at least 9.00 a.m.

'Mm, that sounds lovely.' I rolled over to face him, basking in his morning green eyes, until he closed them placing a kiss on my forehead.

'How are you feeling?' he asked.

I crinkled my face and stretched out my arms, releasing myself from his snug hold. I placed my hand on my belly. I did feel a little queasy, it was a mix of excitement and hunger.

'I'm excited, maybe nervous, probably both...'

'I think that's pretty normal.' He smiled.

'But today's not about me, what about you? How are you feeling?'

'I'm excited. The Arias are always great, especially once all the formalities are done and you have the dinner and party to look forward to. Plus, it's so great to catch up with all the other artists. It's our annual get together.'

'Room service,' yelled an unknown voice from behind the door. Kas winked at me and jumped out of bed to answer the door in his tartan boxers.

'Who are you, Kas? Making room service appear a mere minute after mentioning breakfast in bed?' I laughed, sitting up straight in bed, wearing nothing but his khaki t-shirt. And then realised what I'd just said.

'Maybe I'm magic,' he said, smiling. I gave an uneasy laugh. He placed a large silver tray in the middle of the bed and slithered himself back underneath the covers.

'This has been a tradition for the last three years, Lisa would have already organised it.' He picked up his phone on the bedside table. 'Yep, 9.30 a.m. on the dot.'

'So, we've got half an hour to ourselves before the craziness of the day starts?'

'That we do,' Kas said biting his bottom lip and placing a slow kiss on mine. 'Can I spend it eating croissants with you?' He smiled as he lifted the lid from the silver tray. 'Are you a sweet or savoury girl, Daphne?'

The large silver tray was filled with intoxicating croissants on the left, wafting sweetness through my nostrils, I heard my stomach rumble. On the right side of the tray there was a bowl of fresh mixed berries, yogurt or maybe it was cream, and layers of cheese and ham. A perfect 'do it yourself' French breakfast in bed.

'They both look so divine...' I almost started drooling. 'I don't know, I'm going to let you choose.'

'First up, savoury,' said Kas as he grabbed a knife from the tray and cut through a warm croissant, laying the insides with ham and cheese. 'For today's stamina.' He handed me the perfectly warm treat and began to make the same for himself. 'Then we can enjoy the sweet.' He said. He smiled, his eyes locked on mine as he bit his bottom lip. I giggled, feeling my cheeks blush. I took a bite from the croissant, just as the front door came bursting open.

'Dapphhhhneeeee, it's show day!' Amy waltzed on in holding

a champagne glass filled with orange juice. Wait, who was I kidding, that was definitely a mimosa. As she entered the room, the whole crew came gliding in behind her, Jack, Lana, Eli, Nolan, Matty, Issy... Jesus, was the concierge going to enter our room too? Oh yes, and there they were, someone from the hotel wheeled in a rack of clothes covered in linen bags, I'm sure they were our dresses.

I pulled the doona up higher, holding it underneath my arms as I realised I wasn't wearing a bra under Kas's shirt.

'What are you guys doing? What time did you start breakfast?' Eli said, slightly slurring as he downed a glass of champagne. 'Where's the bottle love?' He turned to Amy as she smiled, grabbing it out of Lana's hand and passing it to him. Eli didn't even bother to pour himself a glass he took a long swig straight from the bottle.

'Breakfast at 9.30 a.m., that's the usual ritual, isn't it?'

'Oh, we all woke up early and asked for it straight away,' said Jack.

There was another knock on the door. 'Room service.' *What was it now?* I thought.

Nolan, who was standing closest to the door, opened it up. 'Thank you.' He kicked the door closed, as both his hands were full with a tray of orange juice, champagne and two clean glasses.

'What? You haven't even been served your mimosas yet? We're on round two,' Eli said, taking another swig.

'I can't half tell,' Kas muttered under his breath. Nolan walked over to sit the tray over on Kas's bedside table.

'I don't want it right now, thanks mate. You can just sit it over there.' Kas gestured to the desk I'd sat at to meet with Noah.

'More for us then,' Eli said.

'Sorry guys, I just wanted to quickly run over today's schedule if that's okay?' Issy jumped in.

'That's fine Is, go for it,' Kas said, sitting back in bed and taking another bite of the pastry.

'Okay, so I've organised for all the dresses to come into your room, Kas, as we're going to use this room for the girls to get ready. We'll use Matty's room for the boys, so all your tuxes are already in there. We're just on an extra time limit this year because hair and make-up for the girls is going to start at 10:30 a.m.' She paused, speaking like a true manager, flicking through all the details in her phone. 'There are a couple of radio interviews that will be taken in Nolan's room. I'm just going to get Jack and Kas to do those and then hair for the boys starts at 11:30 a.m. We need everyone completely ready for our own press and social media pictures by 1:30 p.m. and the limo will be picking everyone up at 3:15 p.m. ready for a 3:50 p.m. red carpet arrival. Any questions?' she said, looking up from her phone.

Amy stared at Issy with her mouth wide open. 'Issy, you're incredible.'

'Yeah, I don't know where we would be without you Is,' Kas added.

'So, you're all good? There's nothing else that anyone needs right now?'

'We're wonderful! In fact, couldn't be more wonderful,' said Amy.

'Okay, okay it's been wonderful chatting with you all but now we all know our movements... can everyone just give Daphne and I a minute. If you don't mind, I'd love to be able to shower and put on some pants,' said Kas.

Sorry Amy mouthed to me. I smiled back to her as Nolan opened the door.

Kas looked down at his phone, it was 9.46 a.m. 'Sorry ladies, come back in at 10:15. Nolan, I'll meet you in your room ready for interviews then.'

'For sure,' said Nolan

'See you then,' Amy and Alana sung in almost perfect unison.

Everyone left the room with Eli the last to leave, flashing us a lop-sided smile, his eyes looking a little dazed. The door finally closed. I took a deep breath. And Kas downed the final bite of his croissant.

'Eli's already drunk,' Kas said, running his hands through his hair anxiously.

'I did notice that, and Amy's buzzed. But she'll be fine, she will stop drinking when we start getting dressed.'

'Eli, on the other hand, I don't have faith in unfortunately.' Kas sighed.

'It seemed like this was a common occurrence the other night at dinner.' I realised I hadn›t spoken to Kas any further about what had happened that night. Other than the brief conversation with Amy days before, nothing else had been mentioned about his drinking. In the chaos of everything else that was going on. I'd let it slip my mind.

'It is. And it's one that I don't particularly want to have to deal with today.'

'What exactly is it?' I asked. 'Do you know why he does it?' I could tell Kas didn't really want to talk about it, but I felt like I had to enquire further, know more about the situation, purely for Amy's sake. I remember when Levi... my heart slightly sunk as I thought about him. But this time it was different. Like I was simply remembering the past, not an unrequited love. He told me about his friend who went to rehab. His drinking started after his long-term girlfriend had a miscarriage and then left him a month later. I remember Levi telling me that the saddest thing about substance abuse is how it can become the devil of drowning pain. I'd never been exposed to it until then. And even then, I'd only heard of it from a distance.

'I don't think it's anything he is trying to numb if that's what you're thinking...' Kas said, handing me a sweet croissant.

'Are you sure about that?' I asked politely, trying not to delve too deep into issues that weren't mine.

'To be honest, we were all heavy drinkers back in the day, it comes with the territory, I guess. When things started taking off for us, our first tour over five years ago now, it began. It just became the nature of the game.' Kas paused, biting into another croissant. 'But for most of us, it wore off pretty quickly, it wasn't productive, and I felt as though I was numbed out when I wanted to create music and as a whole band, we weren't jamming well together. But Eli, he never stopped. He is lucky it's just alcohol, the industry can be filled with a lot darker substances than that.'

'That doesn't mean that there's not something deeper going beyond the surface for him,' I replied, slightly concerned.

'Yeah, you are right. I guess, I'm just not the person that can help him with it. At the start it was a joke, then we became concerned. We tried to talk to him, getting him professional help. He would stop for a month and then just go back to his old ways.' I watched as Kas's eyes floated elsewhere, as though he was lost in thought, trying to figure out what it was that held Eli down. 'Lately we've just been fed up with him. Nolan usually deals with it. But if I'm completely honest with you, I don't know how much longer I can handle it, it's tearing the band apart.'

'I'm sorry.' I didn't know what else to say.

'You have nothing to apologise for, you're not the drunk idiot I have to work with every day.' Kas smiled, turning around and giving me a kiss on the forehead.

'I know, I guess I'm just sorry for bringing it up today, it's your day, this is meant to be an exciting uplifting day for everyone. A celebration of your music.' I threw my hands up into the air, trying to change the energy in the room.

'Don't worry about that, we're still going to have a great time. I'm excited to have you by my side out there. I just hope Nolan is working hard to keep Eli in line right now. And to be honest, I'm glad I saw him like that this morning, because it is something that we can't ignore anymore.' I bit into my second croissant and Kas pulled back the covers, jumping out of bed. 'Oh they took the bottle of champagne, bastards... can I offer you an orange juice?'

'Thanks.' I smiled as Kas poured the fresh OJ into a champagne glass. I sat staring into his green eyes, sitting up in the most luscious bed, croissant in hand and OJ in the other.

'Are you sure you're okay?' he asked, taking a seat on the edge of the bed.

'Okay? I feel like a queen. Today is... today is a dream come true.'

'Take today in. Every moment, Issy's got it all under control.' I laughed. 'My first awards night went too quick, I was stressed, I didn't know what to say in interviews, everything was just a blur. After that day, I learnt to take it slow, take it all in and just enjoy the moment... and maybe stay off social media till tomorrow, you can read all the fashion reviews then.'

'How many awards do you think you'll win tonight? All 7?' I asked.

Kas laughed. 'Honestly, I don't care. It's just cool to be recognised. Awards for me are just taken with a grain of salt, everyone there deserves it... even the people who don't get nominated. I think we all play an important role in the industry and to music in our own unique ways.'

I sat still, in silence, admiring the polarity of his rockstar appearance and humble heart.

'Now queen, is there anything else I can get you before I hop into the shower?' He grinned and a shiver ran down my spine.

I placed the orange juice down on the bedside table and wiggled deeper into the mattress. 'I'm good thank you, I'm just going to enjoy ten more minutes in the kingdom.'

Chapter 18

'When is your dress going to be here Daphne? We can't wait to see it,' Amy said, as she sat in the corner of the room in her one-shoulder seaweed green dress. It hugged her figure beautifully, with a high split that displayed her left leg.

'Look to the left for me.' Gemma, our makeup and hair artist was fixing a smudge of Amy's eye makeup. Personally, I didn't see what she was talking about, but Gemma was a perfectionist, which for today, I highly appreciated. 'Done,' she said and Amy stood up.

I stood in the corner of the room chewing down on celery and hummus. 'Oh AMY! You look incredible!'

'Doesn't she,' Gemma added. Gemma loved the vibe. She'd made our makeup natural, and my lips were red and bold, almost matching Lana's dress.

Amy walked towards the full-length mirror. 'Oh my gosh, I do look incredible. Daph, you're amazing. I can't believe I'm wearing this dress.'

She walked towards me, holding her arms out towards me but I held her back. 'Oh no, that's pure silk,' I said, staring at her dress. 'Let's not get any creases until later tonight.'

'Oh, you're so right, I'm going to stand as still as I can. I'm not going to eat or drink until the red carpet is over.'

'Good idea,' I nodded, dipping another stick of celery into the hummus. Trying to chew without moving my perfectly painted face.

'So, when is Sophia getting here?' said Amy.

'Knock, knock,' I heard Heath's voice on the other side of the door.

'That will be her now,' I said as I opened to door, chewing down the last of my celery stick.

'Hello darling,' Heath said, as he and Colin entered the room both holding the puffy package that was perfectly zipped up in linen.

'Hey. You can hang it up there.' I pointed to the now empty clothes rack that the girls' dresses had been wheeled in on earlier today.

'Sophia sends her deepest apologies; she got caught up with another client, but she will be at the red carpet to watch the show.'

'Oh, that's fine,' I replied softly.

'But we're here to dress you, what time do you need to be ready for photos? I feel like we're running a little late.'

'Yeah, I think you're meant to be downstairs in 15 minutes, I was given strict instructions on when to be finished by,' said Gemma.

'Oh, we better get you in this...' Heath's jaw dropped as the bathroom door swung open. 'Oh. My. God. Who are you?'

Lana appeared in the most perfect red mini dress I had ever seen in my life. Red taffeta wrapped around her neck and stopped at the top of her thigh. It was exactly as I'd imagined, the whole look of tonight had contrast all over it. It was risky. But the true fashion girls would understand my vibe. It was rockstar classy.

Amy ran to meet Lana in front of the full-length mirror. 'We look... sexy, classy.'

'We look like no one would fuck with us.' Lana smiled, loving her new look.

'Daphne you're a freaking genius, it's like LA rockstar 90's meets...'

'The Koras?' I jumped in.

'Exactly,' she said.

'You're part of the red carpet crew?' Colin stared at Amy and Lana in disbelief.

Amy and Lana swung around to the boys, but no one spoke.

'Daphne! What the fuck have you done?' Heath yelled.

'What do you mean?' I muttered, blood drained from my face.

'This is not what Sophia asked you to do... Oh, she's going to be so pissed.' Heath wrapped his arms around the front of his body and began to pace up and down the room.

'Why?' I said, my voice began to shake.

'Yeah, Why?' Amy butted in. 'I don't know what you're looking at, but I think I look the best I ever have thanks to Daphne!'

'Didn't Sophia give you a list of designers to work with?' he said, his voice riddled with fear.

'Yes, but they only made neutrals... and I have this friend Noah... well he wasn't a friend, but now we're friends...'

'These dresses are designed by Noah Still?'

'Yes,' I replied, still trying to figure out what the problem was.

'Daphne, are you stupid? Sophia can't be seen alongside Noah Still; he's trying to take over Australia. Australia is Sophia's fashion business, no one else's. We don't want him here... Sophia's going to die when her finest piece is on display next to his,' said Heath, biting his lips together, his breath shallow.

'But... Noah is a fan of Sophia's, he wants to meet her,' I said, half choking on my words.

'Daphne... I'll tell you one thing right now, and it will be the biggest lesson you'll ever learn. No one is friends in this industry.'

My heart started to rise up through my chest, and I felt a lump forming at the base of my throat. Oh no, it wasn't a lump it was real vomit this time. I tried to run to the bathroom but couldn't in time. I turned to the small bin in the corner of the room, throwing up what seemed like a croissant but tasted like hummus.

'Oh my god Daph, are you okay?' Amy ran over and leaned down to rub my back.

I curled up on my knees, head in the bin. I took a deep breath. 'Don't lean down Amy, your dress.' I composed myself, the sickness stopped, and I stood back up. 'I'm fine, I'm fine. I just... I've really fucked up.'

'I don't know what you're talking about Daphne, everyone looks great,' Gemma consoled me, handing me bunch of tissues and flashing a death stare towards Heath.

'No, she really fucked up,' said Colin.

'Quick, we're running out of time, we've got to get you dressed and then leave. Because as far as I'm concerned, this is your mess and we're not getting involved. Colin and I are not losing our jobs over this. When Sophia asks us if we knew, we're going to pretend we didn't see anyone other than Daphne.' Heath scowled.

'As far as we're concerned, you're not even here now. Help her get dressed and leave,' Amy said sternly.

'My pleasure.' Heath unzipped the linen bag, and I stripped off my rob. The boys pulled out the dress and I reached my arms out to hold onto their shoulders as I stepped into the middle of the dress and the men pulled it up. Pinning together the corset with a little more force than last time. The boys took a step back, looking up and down making sure the dress was sitting perfectly, then without saying anything, they left the room. Slamming the door shut behind them.

My eyes started to well and my stomach churned harder underneath the tight dress. My body dropped on the bed as the ball gown flew up either side of me, almost covering the whole bed. This was my big shot, and I think I'd fucked it all up.

'Hey Daph, don't cry, you can't ruin your make-up,' Amy pleaded.

'Yeah, besides those guys don't even know what they're talking about... you've made us all look amazing, wait till tomorrow's red carpet review—have you seen how you look right now, you're going to be the front cover of every best dressed article,' Lana said.

'Hey Daph, it's going to be fine. You look incredible, the girls look incredible. It's going to be great,' Gemma pipped in. 'Please don't cry, I really don't have time to fix your make-up.' I took deep breaths, trying to hold back tears. There had only been a few times in my life I'd felt incredibly anxious and overwhelmed, most of them seemed to be of late, but this one was the worst. I started to feel my body shake.

'I'm so sorry girls, but I've got to go and double check the boy's hair,' Gemma said, standing in the doorway.

'That's fine, we need to go down too. I just need to calm down, put my shoes on and we'll meet you down there.'

'Hey, are you okay?' Amy asked after Gemma left as she and Lana grabbed my shoes, each helping me put one on underneath all my layers.

'What if this all goes wrong? What if I have done the worst thing and I make an absolute full out of myself? What if I can never show my face again. What if I make a fool out of Kas on his night?'

'Hey Daph, that's not going to happen,' said Lana.

'How do you know?'

'Because you're incredibly talented, and you've done everything under the purest intentions. When you have a creative vision as strong as yours, I think it's put there for a reason, and other people are going to see it too.'

My lips cracked a small smile, remembering Kas's almost identical words from this morning.

'One thing you do need to be careful of is how incredibly talented and gifted you are Daph...what you say comes true remember. So, think positive, stay positive and the best is going to happen.'

'Yes,' Lana agreed a little too loudly, 'like your name all over the front of the Sydney Herald.'

'Fuck the Sydney Herald, Lana, Daphne's name's going in Vogue.'

I smiled, but I couldn't speak, scared the tears would still fall. I kept my breathing deep and slow.

'Besides, who does that bitch think she is? If you're asked to style something, then you style it. Does she know who you are? Girl, your creativity wasn't meant to stay within the lines, or in this case, the list of fucking neutrals,' said Amy.

I laughed. 'Thanks girls. Besides tonight isn't about us, it's about the boys.'

'Girl, I don't know about you but I'm wearing Noah Still, so I'm going to make tonight as much about me as I can.'

Amy opened the door fabulously and Lana helped me to my feet.

◆ ◆ ◆

'You look fucking incredible,' Kas whispered in my ear as each of us posed in our group shots down an alleyway with a dark brick wall background across the road from the hotel.

'You don't scrub up too bad yourself,' I whispered under my breath in between smiles.

He kissed my cheek; I felt my heart quicken as the camera flashed. Everyone looked exactly how I had imagined.

'Okay ladies, you can take a break now, I just need some of the guys,' the photographer said. Kas kissed my cheek lightly again; aware he couldn't wreck my make-up. The girls and I walked over to join Issy, who was standing at the entrance of the alleyway.

'Daphne, you look like it could be your wedding day,' said Lana.

'Well, I guess today could be the beginning or very tragic ending of something.'

'Don't be like that. It's the beginning girl and you know it.'

'Eli, would you stand up straight?' Nolan yelled to Eli behind the photographer. I don't know how the photographer stayed so poised; Nolan was practically screaming in his ear.

'Do you want to come inside ladies? Save your dresses, the limo should only be 20 minutes away,' Issy said, pointing towards the entrance of the hotel. She'd booked the ground floor boardroom for the boys to do more press shots and create social's content all afternoon. One by one we all pilled in there, trying not to move too quickly, keeping everything intact.

The far-right wall of the room was filled with fruit, chicken salad wraps and quiches. An ice bucket was filled with beers, champagne and fresh orange juice. Everyone had already gotten into it.

'I think I might finally have a mimosa.' I looked over at Issy pouring three glasses.

'Of course, how are you feeling? Nerves kicking in?' Issy asked as she handed me my glass.

'Yeah, they are a little bit.' I took the glass in one hand and held out my other exposing my tiny shakes.

'Oh honey, it's going to be fine, everyone looks fabulous, and the carpet will be over before you know it.'

'I know, I know,' I said before downing the glass. It wasn't the carpet that I was worried about, it was Sophia's face, staring at me from the carpet, her reaction, her power, what she could do to me... would she really be that mad? Could she block and delete my fashion career forever?

I won't have to deal with Sophia tonight. I tried to imbed the thought, but my anxiety had already taken over my body. I couldn't help but not feel worried about what was going to happen.

'Oh no, I don't want one thanks,' Amy said as Issy handed her a mimosa.

'Amy are you okay?' I asked, laughing. Out of all the years I'd known Amy, I don't think I'd once seen her ever refuse a glass of alcohol. Issy placed Amy's glass in my shaking hand. I shrugged and took it. *They were mimosa's, half the strength,* I thought.

'Don't worry, I'll catch up. I just think I might need to be the one holding up Eli on the red carpet.'

Issy sighed out loudly. 'He has been cut off and given a Berocca and Hydrolyte. He has also been strictly warned that he isn't allowed to speak during any carpet interview. You'll be fine love.'

I watched Amy sit down, crossing her legs underneath the seaweed green dress. Her head hung down towards the ground in front of her, twisting the ring on her right hand. Completely lost in thought. I wanted to say so much, but not in front of Issy.

'Ahhh, you're all back,' Issy said. I followed her gaze, looking towards the door, as all the boys walked in.

'Are you okay love? Double parked?' Kas said, walking behind me. He squeezed my shoulders, and kissed the side of my neck. I loved it when he did that. I'd never felt the full body tingles I heard my mother talk about when it came to men, until now.

I finished the final sip of my first glass, placing it down on the table next to me. 'I'm great... how are you?'

'I'm ready.' He smiled, gazing into my eyes.

'Okay, limo's out front,' Issy said from across the room as though she'd just heard our conversation. 'Let's go.' Issy took charge of everyone, opening the boardroom doors as we made our way through reception towards a ridiculously large limo that was parked directly at the front door.

'Okay I need everyone in order, well I need everyone in backwards,' Issy laughed.

'What?' Jack laughed alongside Issy.

'Daphne, Kas, you guys get in first because you are going to be the last to walk onto the carpet. Followed by Matty, Amy, Eli, Lana and then Jack...'

'After you.' Kas helped grab the back of my dress as I leaned into the limo, sliding along to the far seat, with Kas sitting up close next to me, half smothered by the material of my dress.

Issy stood on the sidewalk, leaning into the limo. 'Okay guys, this is where I leave you. If there's anything else you need tonight, I'm on call. I'll be watching from the comfort of my room.'

'You've been freaking amazing Issy, thank you,' Jack said, and everyone cheered Issy's name. She really was the angel of The Koras.

'Go win boys!' Issy slammed the door shut.

'Yeiwwww!' Kas yelled back as the driver pulled away.

'Champagne?' Matty picked up the bottle sitting next to him.

'It's a ten-minute drive, better wait.' I saw Kas's eyes narrow in on Matty. One look said it all and Matty placed the bottle back down.

'Here he bloody is, stopping the party before it's even started,' Eli slurred, pushing himself over the top of Matty to grab the champagne bottle. Matty pressed it down hard into its holder, with so much force, drunk Eli couldn't set it free with one arm.

'You all fucking suck.' Eli sat back down in his seat. 'What if my girl wants a glass of champagne, can she have one?'

'I'm fine, I'll have one when we get there,' said Amy. She wouldn't look at him, staring down at her Louis.

'Babe, enjoy yourself, that's what we're here for.' Eli placed his arm around Amy and whispered in her ear.

'Thanks, but I'm fine, I just want to wait until I get there.'

Eli snapped his arm back from around Amy and reached into his jacket, pulling out a small silver flask.

'Eli, are you fucking serious?! You're drunk, no you're not drunk, you're well and truly passed drunk, you're a mess,' Kas growled. I had been yet to see him like this, his whole body tensed.

'Thanks for pointing that out Mr. fucking perfect. But isn't this what it's all meant to be about, this is the rockstar life isn't it? Get drunk, play, fuck.' He grabbed onto Amy's thigh, and I could feel the shiver down her spine from across the limo. Lana and I met eyes with Amy. Lana went to move to sit between the two, but Amy shook her head and waved her back down. She squeezed Eli's hand, pulling his hand off her leg and placing it back down on his, resting her hand lightly on top of it. Her face dropped and her jaw clenched, looking away from Lana and me.

'You all used to be fun.' He waved the flask around, pointing to Kas and then to Matt and Jack. 'What the fuck happened to you.'

'Eli, you can't go out on the red carpet like this. You do realise how much we're about to be pictured, and like Kas said, you're a fucking mess. You can't walk the carpet. I'm calling Nolan,' said Jack sternly, as he reached for his phone in his pant pocket.

The tension in the limo made my heart pound fast through my chest, raising the heat of my body. I grabbed onto my left hand with my right as it started to shake, I wasn't too sure if I was going to vomit or cry, either way I wanted to run, hide. Walk away from this whole thing. Kas watched me grabbing hold of my own shaking hand and held both of mine tightly. Leaning in closer towards me, he gently kissing my ear.

'I'm sorry.'

I caught his gaze and shook my head as if to say, *don't be. None of this is your fault.* Eli took a long sip from his flask, making sure everyone around him was looking at him. 'Go ahead mate, call Nolan. What's he going to do?'

Jack's phone was pressed up to his ear, but Nolan didn't seem to be answering. *Where was Nolan?* I thought. The last time I saw him he was on the phone in boardroom.

'He's going to organise for you to be escorted for disorderly conduct as soon as the limo pulls up, because there is no way in hell you're walking the carpet or accepting any awards like that.'

'Fuck off, I'm part of this band. I have just as many rights on our contracts as you do Jack.' Eli took another long swig from his flask, surely it was going to be empty soon. Eli's eyes locked on Jack's as Jack held the phone solid to his ear. Eli jumped out of his seat, almost side swiping Amy, knocking Jack's phone down onto the floor and spilling the remainder of his flask all over Lana's legs.

Lana jumped from the shock. 'Oh my god.'

'Did it get on the dress?' I gasped.

'No, no it's fine,' she reassured me.

The limo stopped, and the car door opened.

'Pat your legs down Lana, it's going to be fine.' Amy reached over to help Lana.

'Omg I'm going to smell like fucking whisky.'

'Ready guys?' A man with dark glasses and a black suit leaned into the limo, then spoke into a microphone on his chest, 'I've got The Koras.' He looked back into limo. 'Okay let's go.'

Kas grabbed my hand. Jack looked at Lana and then Amy. 'Okay, smiles on. It's game time.'

Chapter 19

I stepped out of the limo, smiling, but my eyes were scared. I squeezed Kas's hand so hard my knuckles, and probably his too, were white. He gently kissed my cheek.

'Everyone's out, okay let's go.' The same man who told us to get out of the limo placed his hand in the middle of my back and pushed me forward. It was all such a blur. A literal blur. Lights flashed from every direction.

'The Koras! Kas! Matty!' I heard people yelling but I couldn't see any faces. My foot hit the red carpet. It was full of people. Colours, faces, screams from every direction. I just had to stand straight and smile.

A tall thin woman with straight black hair and a black pant suit approached us. 'Hey Kas,' she said.

'Hey,' he said back, hardly moving his photogenic smile. Mindful of the constant flashes.

'Okay, guys first up, I need you to pose here.' The woman pointed to a space on the carpet just in front of the Aria backdrop. We all made our assigned poses that we had practiced back in the boardroom earlier that day. As I stood still, smiling with one of Kas's arms wrapped around my waist, Sophia came into my mind. I wondered where she stood in the crowd, I wondered what she was thinking, now the big reveal was in motion.

'Okay, you've got to speak with Channel V and HIIT 102 up here on your left.' The woman pointed us in the direction. I followed Kas's lead. It was decided that Kas and Matty would speak at all the interviews, but the girls had to go along and linger in the background, in case we got asked who we were wearing.

Kas let go of my hand as he and Matty walked towards the presenters, a curly haired man threw a microphone straight into Kas's face. I was only standing a metre away, lingering next to Lana. Lana and Amy stood like models, faces poised and smiling. We all met each others' eyes, and the girls' smiles were contagious. I couldn't help but let out a giggle. The lights and people surrounding us was overwhelming, the thought of Sophia in the crowd still sat nervously on my heart. But standing here, with Lana and Amy and now Kas. There was nowhere else I would rather be, and no one else I would rather be here with.

'You guys have been the centre of the Australian music scene this year, and you've been travelling everywhere, how's road life been treating you?' the young man asked.

'We've been having a blast; the shows have been amazing. The energy in the venues has been unreal. Honestly, if you told us three years ago that we would be here now, I probably would have laughed in your face,' Kas replied.

'I'm pretty sure I did tell you that Kas. Back in my radio days I remember interviewing you when your first song, Iridescent? hit radio, that was longer than three years ago, and I remember betting that you guys where about to hit the big scene.'

'Did I laugh in your face?'

'Yeah, I think you did.' All the men laughed.

I watched Kas's game face, he was so well spoken, humble and even a little awkward and shy. It was cute to see him like this. I wondered how long this carpet would go for, how sore his cheeks would be from smiling, and how many times he would have to answer the same questions.

'Did I hear you have an American tour coming up too?' The man pointed the microphone back in Kas's face again. I felt my heart sink a little... I had completely forgotten about the American tour.

'We do, it's in three months. I don't have all the dates right now, but if you head to our socials or website, all the details and tickets are there. We're really excited to be heading over to the States.'

'Now you're nominated for seven awards tonight including Artist of the Year, how are you feeling?'

'Honestly, I'm trying not to think about it. I think being nominated is an unbelievable recognition and we're all so grateful for Australia getting around us. But everyone here tonight is equally worthy. So we're just stocked that we get to be a part of something like this and we're excited that we get to enjoy a fun night.'

'Can you spill any tour secrets? Have you got anything about any of the other band members you'd love to tell us? What is it like to be on the road with The Koras.'

I thought about Eli when he asked that question. Shit. *Where was Eli?* I looked around, he was standing right behind me, his arm around Amy, his eyes were a little bloodshot in the bright lights. You could tell he was drunk; his head was all over the place, staring at everyone left to right of the carpet. But no one seemed to be paying any attention back to him, it was probably a good thing.

I looked back at the interviewer, Matty started answering the question.

'This tour has been a little bit different, because all the boys, other than me, decided to get girlfriends. So it's just been little old me by myself, while the boys are all hidden away and loved up.' Matty sighed, then grinned.

'Actually, I'd love to know what Matty has been getting up to,' Kas started to joke, giving the interviewer some banter to play with, 'because we actually never see him. I bet he has a thousand wild stories that none of us know about.'

'And no one's ever going to,' Matty chuckled back.

'I did see you've brought three gorgeous women here with you tonight… Since it is a red carpet can we ask the lovely ladies who you're wearing tonight?'

Kas turned around holding his hand out, pulling me over to the interviewer, Lana and Amy followed me close behind. The interviewer placed the microphone in front of my face.

'I'm wearing a Lady Meyers Original,' I said, taking a step back and spinning around, giving the cameraman the perfect shot.

'This is Noah Still,' said Amy, smiling perfectly, dazzling her eyes directly into the camera and standing back towards me.

'And what is this little red number? This is for sure the show stealer tonight.' The man flashed Lana a little too cheeky smile, I wondered if anyone else saw.

'This is a Noah Still custom piece as well,' she said into the microphone and then stood back next to me.

'And everything all the boys and girls are wearing tonight was styled by my gorgeous girl, Daphne.' Kas grabbed my hand and kissed my cheek. In that very moment, it didn't matter what Sophia thought. Kas had just announced to the world, that I was his girl.

'Okay, time to move along.' The thin woman reappeared, and together, we re-joined the carpet, walking a further three meters down before being asked to stop for photos again. We huddled back into our usual pose.

'Lady in red, lady in red—who made your dress,' I heard someone within the flashing crowd called up, but I kept my photo face intact, breathing slow, holding onto Kas's tight grip around my waist.

'Let's do a funny one,' I heard Eli, who was standing beside Amy to my left, call out, and then snort and laugh. 'Yeah strike a real fucking pose,' he said.

I turned to my left as I felt Amy move next to me. Eli had wrapped his arm around her, and she was trying to pull away gracefully, still smiling, super aware of the number of cameras that were surrounding us.

'C'mon darling, strike a pose,' Eli slurred close in Amy's ear. He was pulling on her harder.

'Don't,' she shouted. I swung around. Pulling myself free from Kas's hold. Eli was pulling Amy towards him and pushing on her back, as if to mimic he was bending her over the bathroom sink, like Amy had given me the visuals of days before. Eli started laughing. Amy was stuck, being pictured in front of anyone. She kept a smile on her face but fear flooded her eyes and her jaw clenched tight.

'Eli let her go!' I screamed, walking in front of Amy, hoping my dress would block her from the cameras view. He grabbed hold of her so hard, her feet weren't touching the ground anymore.

'Whatcha going to do Cinderella.' He laughed harder.

'Eli, let her go. Now.' I gritted under my teeth as I felt the heat raise. I forgot where I was. I forgot about the cameras. I forgot about Sophia fucking Myers. I forgot about being a good little girl on the red carpet. All I wanted to do was hurt Eli. And to get him as far away from Amy as soon as possible. I wanted to scream, I wanted to hurt him so bad. How dare he touch her like that.

'Okay.' He smiled and dropped Amy to the floor. I felt her fall on her hands and knees and land on the left corner of my dress.

I had cracked, my final barrier gone. I launched at him. Taking a forceful step forward, with Amy on my dress I felt the tear... I felt something hit my cheek ....

I felt myself fall...

Chapter 20

'Daph, Daph, can you hear us?'

I heard the call, but I couldn't see anyone. Someone grabbed my hand. I flickered my eyes open. Amy and Lana's faces where right in front of mine.

'Oh, Daph you're okay!' Lana sighed.

'You had us so worried.' Amy's eyes welled.

Was she crying? Why was she crying? I blinked a couple times, the lights where so bright, I felt naked... where was I? I reached my arms out to stretch, looking down at my body, something was connected to my finger. Fuck, I was... I jumped up, looking around the room.

'Yep, she's well and truly awake now.' A strange woman stood beside me, taking my hand. 'Hello Daphne, I'm Tabitha. I'm a nurse here at St. Vincent's hospital. You've taken a large fall. We're here to look after you and make sure you're okay... I'm just going to grab your doctor okay. Is there anything else I can get for you right now? I shook my head, letting go of her hand. Tabitha smiled kindly and quickly walked out of the room.

'What happened?' I said, turning back to Lana and Amy, who were standing at the end of my bed. I could feel the panic well and truly setting in now.

'Do you not remember?' Lana asked, moving to sit beside me.

'I remember a fight... I remember Kas holding my hand.' I pulled back the sheets, I was wearing a blue hospital robe,

'Where's my dress? Did Sophia see it?'

Lana leaned in placing the back of her hand on my forehead.

'Are you checking my temperature? Seriously, what happened?' I asked. I felt my left hand starting to shake again. I grabbed it with my right and looked down. 'My hands, they were shaking in the limo, we were in the limo, what am I doing here?' I felt tears start to fall down my cheeks, Amy wiped them away with a tissue. 'Kas, where's Kas?'

Tabitha walked back into the room, holding the door open behind her for another woman dressed in navy blue scrubs and holding a clipboard.

'Hello Daphne, I'm Moreen, I'm going to be your doctor during your stay here.'

'While I'm here? How long am I here for?'

'I'll answer all of your questions as soon as I can, I just need you to answer some for me first okay?' Moreen replied softly.

I nodded; she took a seat down next to me on the chair. 'Are you in any pain at all?'

'I... I don't think so, I feel a little dizzy and I have a bit of a headache,' I said.

'Have you tried moving around at all? Could you just try and move your legs for me?'

I circled my feet and kicked my legs, starting to get extremely frustrated why I was doing this with still no explanation.

'Perfect, and do you mind just moving your torso to the left and to the right.'

I sat up straighter in the bed, turning from left and then towards Tabitha on my right.

'Yeah.' I winced. 'My back does hurt, and my left hip is killing me.'

'Do you know why you're in hospital right now?' she asked slowly. I shook my head.

'What's the last thing that you remember Daphne?' Her eyes

observed my every moment.

'The last thing I remember was, being at the Aria's, the three of us, with the guys and Kas. Where's Kas?' I breathed shallow as something in my back began to hurt. 'The reviews? Are there any yet? Where's my dress? Has anyone heard from Sophia' I looked up at the girls, but neither of them spoke.

I looked back towards my hip, lifting my hospital gown. More tears fell from my face as I looked down at my black and blue skin a large dressing sat over my hip, I could see the blood stains underneath the white cotton bandage.

'Can someone please tell me what happened,' I said in between the tears.

'Daph, you went to save me.' Tears started falling from Amy's eyes as she rubbed my shin.

'Was the last memory you have in the limo?' said Lana.

'Yes,' I replied nervously.

'Daphne, you've had a large fall and an impact wound, not to mention suffering concussion and shock. Don't give yourself a hard time about remembering anything right now, it will come back in time.'

'Did I trip out of the car?' I looked at Lana.

'No. Do you remember Eli in the car drunk?' Lana said slowly. I nodded.

'Things got a little heated on the red carpet. He started pushing and pulling Amy and well, you saw what was happening and stepped in.'

I felt a shiver down my spine and Moreen placed her hand on top of mine, grounding my uneasy feelings.

'Eli had a hold of Amy and he dropped her on the corner of your dress. You stepped towards him, I don't know what you were going to do, but as you did, the skirt of your dress tore and fell. At the same time Eli hit you... he hit you hard, in the side of the head, which explains the bruising... and you fell...'

I wiggled my hand out from underneath Moreen's and touched the right side of my head. I hadn't seen my face, I knew it was aching. I wonder how bad it looked.

'Where's Kas?'

'All the boys had to go straight to the police station to provide statements. Eli is currently being held in custody for assault,' said Lana as Amy tightly grabbed my shin.

'What happened to you was a very violent act, the police are here wanting to talk to you to. But I don't care about them, I care about your health and your welfare right now. I'm going to tell them to wait,' Moreen said.

'Everything they need to see is all over every news platform ever created,' said Amy.

'What?' I looked at Amy.

'There were a hundred cameras there filming the whole thing.'

'My ass is on the news?'

Lana and Amy nodded in unison, unsure what to say.

'I'm so sorry,' Amy cried. 'It's a horrible video to watch, I don't ever want you to see it.'

'And I'd advise not watching it Daphne, at least not for the time being. I would really love to organise our phycologist here to come and speak with you as well,' Moreen said sternly, half looking at the girls.

Let me go home.

'I don't want to be here, I don't want to be dealing with this right now, can I just go home,' I cried, unsure how I felt about it all, wishing I could take it all back. This god damn power, the last couple of weeks. Everything.

'I'm going to need to monitor you for a couple more days, I can't have you going home yet, I'm so sorry. But you're very lucky Daphne, that fall could have been fatal.'

Wait what? Everything I'd ever thought or said over the past couple of weeks had happened... but this time...

Let me go home.

'Can you please let me go home, I'll be fine. Just organise for all of us to go home ASAP,' I pleaded with Moreen.

'I'm sorry Daphne, as soon as I can, I will,' Moreen replied. 'Now I'm going to go and let the police know that they won't be speaking with you today. But I'm sure they will want to speak to you girls very soon.' Moreen looked towards Amy and Lana. 'Tabitha will organise you some food, I'm sure you're starving. I'll be back to check in on you soon,' she said as both women left the room.

I waited a few seconds until I knew Tabatha and Moreen where down the hall, rustling around in the bed, trying to get myself comfortable. 'It's gone guys, it's gone... my powers gone. I can't get us out of this one and look at where we are.'

'Wait what?' Amy said, wiping her own tears, and fixing me with a worried look. 'How do you know it's gone?'

'Did you not see what happened? I asked, I thought... she still didn't let us go home... I just want to go home; don't you guys want to go home?'

'We want to go home too girl, but I'm worried about you... I want you to get better... I want to make sure that everything is going to be okay first,' Lana said, speaking to me as though I was one of her patients.

'How bad is it? The media? The incident...'

'Bad enough to be the front cover of every pop culture news station... and regular news station around the world,' said Lana. 'There's also news crews everywhere outside of the hospital right now.'

'This is all my fault.' Amy hung her head. 'We shouldn't be here right now.'

'Amy, this isn't your fault. This isn't anyone's fault. Please don't blame yourself,' I said.

'No, it is. I should have known it was going to get worse. I never wanted anyone to get hurt, that wasn't what this was about. I just wanted us to have fun. That was all I wanted, some time away with my girls. Who knew when we were ever going to experience a trip like this again? I should have said something the first time that you called out his drinking and his behaviour,' said Amy in between tears. My heart panged. The last thing I wanted was for Amy to put the blame on herself.

'Amy, did Eli ever hurt you?' Lana asked.

Amy gulped down. 'I mean, he was always rougher, you know, on the nights he drank a lot. But today, something had changed in him. He pushed me against the wall before we came down to your room at breakfast. I don't think that he had slept last night, he stayed out and when I woke up he was sitting on the end of the bed stinking like a distillery.' Amy paused, gulping down more tears as she looked down, her bottom lip trembling. Lana grabbed hold of her hand. 'He pushed me against the wall of our room and held me there, he told me that the three of us were there to make the boys' night better. So, we better act nice and play pretty, and then he stormed down towards Kas's room. I should have told you he wasn't safe to be around at all today. I'm so sorry.' Amy wept.

'No, no Amy this isn't your fault at all, and you're not allowed to feel guilty for this. I won't allow it,' said Lana, squeezing Amy's hand tighter.

'We love you, and none of this is because of you at all, I can guarantee you that,' I said, my body felt too tight to reach down towards her. But my eyes met hers and she let out a soft smile.

We sat still. No one spoke but I knew what was going through my best friends' heads. *What are we doing here, how did it get to this... it was just meant to be a bit of fun.*

How naive I had been. I had been given this power, this gift, and what had I done? I'd gone and created something of no substance, no meaning, never thinking about the comedown.

Never thinking about how it would affect all of us.

'I'm with Daphne, I say we get out of here,' said Amy.

'And how are we going to do that? What about Daphne's fucking brain? said Lana.

'I don't know Lana, you're the nurse, maybe you could monitor her.' Amy scowled at Lana.

'Or maybe we could safely get transferred to a hospital back home?' I said seriously—I knew that was what I wanted. 'Do you think anyone back home will know about this?'

'Daph, the whole world already knows, I'm surprised you're not receiving phone calls from everyone you've ever known right now.'

'Fuck, my mum. She's on top of every news article… She would've seen it.'

'The hospital asked to call her. I said I would, I just haven't got around to it yet. This has all happened really quickly.'

'Don't worry, I'll call her… where is my phone?' I asked the girls before Lana interrupted.

'Kas is calling me…' Lana said, as we all stared down at her phone sitting on the bed, watching it ring. 'I'm not answering it.'

Seeing his name, knowing he was with Eli… I felt numb. Not just because I couldn't remember, or because right now it hurt to think about anything too much. I felt numb because I didn't know who I was anymore, I didn't know what the power had made me become… I didn't know how I felt about Kas anymore, or his world. I didn't know anything. Physically I was hurting, emotionally I was numb.

The phone rang out and a woman appeared through the door. 'I'm just dropping off some food, love,' she said, not introducing herself.

Lana took the tray out of her hands and sat it on my side table. 'He's calling again.'

'Answer it, maybe he can help get us home,' I said.

Lana, nodding, taking a deep breath, pressed the green on her screen and held the phone to her ear. Amy and I were silent, staring at her.

'Hello,' Lana said, reserved.

'Lana, hey, what's going on? Is she okay? Please tell me she's okay?' He was loud through the phone; I could hear his every word.

Lana turned to walk away. 'What do you think Kas? You saw what happened? Of course, she's not okay! How fucking dare he, how fucking dare he touch her like that. I will never, never ever let him live this down.' Lana's voice turned into a wail; I watched the anger shake her thin body.

'Please just tell me that she's awake. Lana is she awake?'

Was he crying? His voice became faint and muffled, I couldn't hear anything else he was saying through the phone. Lana paused.

'Yes, she's awake, but no, no and no. She needs to get home; we all need to go home.'

'Let me talk to him,' I said to Lana while she stood with her back turned to me, as though I couldn't hear their conversation. 'Let me talk to him.'

Lana swung around, flashing me her doe caring eyes, shaking her head.

'Let me speak to him.' I raised my voice at her.

'Daph, no.' Lana's eyes pleaded with me.

'Let me speak to him,' I said again, looking directly in her eyes.

Lana's angry shaking arm slowly dropped from her ear as she held out the phone towards me. Her eyes not leaving my gaze. I grabbed hold of the phone, took a deep breathe and sank deeper into the pillows behind my back, holding the phone to my ear.

'Daph?' he said, he was crying. I could hear every crack in his voice.

'Yea…' My voice was soft, trying not to give away any emotion.

But I know I'd already failed at that. I scrunched my face, trying to stop more tears from flowing, but it was hopeless.

'I'm sorry, I'm so sorry. He's locked away, he's not coming out I promise. I promise you we will keep him away for as long as it takes...'

'I don't want to talk about it. I just want to go home. I need to stay in hospital, but I just want to be transferred home.'

'Of course, I'll come to the hospital now, we'll organise this all for you.'

'No.' I wept. 'I just want this to be smooth, I just want to get home without anyone trying to chuck a microphone in my face or get a scoop, I can't have you here right now. I don't want to see you.'

'Daph—'

'Just please get Issy to give Lana a call.'

'I've spoken to Issy, she's already on her way to the hospital. Daph let me see you... please. Tell me if there's anything at all I can do for you right now. I don't care what it is, let me do it.'

'I just want to go home,' I repeated.

'We'll get you home, I promise, and no one will know where you are, you'll be safe.' He paused. His pause pounded my heart, hearing his sniffles and his croaky voice. 'I should have never dragged you into this. I should have never even let him into the car let alone out of it... If I could take today back, I would.'

'I can't remember it, but I already want to forget it, all of it.'

'Daph.'

I hung up the phone, I couldn't bare to hear his voice anymore and the tears became so deep, the pain contracting my chest and hurting my back. I wanted to crawl up into a ball, but my body hurt too much.

'Daphne.' Issy ran into the hospital room right on que, holding an obnoxiously large bunch of flowers. She placed them down on the side-table next to my food that I'd yet to touch. 'Oh Daphne,

I would have never dreamed that this would happened,' she said as she sat down on the chair next to me, dragging it in close. 'If it's any consolation, I quit. I told Kas moments ago that I'm not working for them anymore. There's no way in hell I'm fixing their PR drama, and as far as I'm concerned Eli can stay locked up forever.'

'That's just what Kas said.'

'Kas? Have you been speaking to him?'

'Yes briefly, I asked him to call you. But he said he already had.'

'We all really want to get home Issy, I'm sure the hospital will let Daphne be transferred. But we just need a quick and comfortable escape without anyone knowing where we are,' said Lana.

Issy nodded. 'Get a transfer approved and I'll get you a plane. No one will know. News reporters will still be filming out the front of the hospital and you'll be back home. Let me make a couple of calls.' She reached out, resting her hand on my arm, before standing up, grabbing her phone and walking back out of the room.

'Can I get you something to eat?' said Lana, moving Issy's flowers and opening the tray of food. It was a chicken salad wrap. The freshest hospital food I'd seen.

'I'm fine for the moment, thanks though.'

'I don't know if you need to be mad at Kas,' said Amy.

'I love you both,' I said adjusting myself slightly on the bed, 'but I don't think anyone should be telling me how I should be right now.'

Amy bit her lip and stared at me with apologetic eyes.

Tabitha opened the door, eyes honing in on Amy and Lana immediately. 'The police want to chat to you girls.'

Chapter 21

8 weeks later

'Are you sure you're okay? You know I don't have to go away yet.'

'Are you kidding me? You've worked your ass off for me lately, one week is going to be fine. You should take two... everything is under control; you don't have to worry,' I said.

Lisa stared at me wide eyed, I think she was assessing my mental state. 'Seriously you have no idea how excited I am to be back at work... I need this, I really do. I need to feel normal again.' I didn't even know what normal was anymore. Whatever it was before the last few months, I knew that life was never going to go back to that.

I opened the door. 'Now go, please enjoy the break, please don't think about me, please don't call me, please get a massage, swim in the ocean, bake your skin and I'll see you when you get back.'

'Thanks, Daph.' She smiled, 'But if anything goes wrong—'

'If anything goes wrong, it will be all be under control.' I leaned in to give her a hug and then waved her out the front door of Duskk, walking back behind the computer to finish the days admin. It was my second day back at work.

The four walls of what used to be my favourite place felt different. Who was I kidding, the whole town felt different. I felt different. I was seeing a psychologist every fortnight. It was the doctors' orders after the whole ordeal. My psychologist told me trauma creates change, a change we don't always choose. But we have the power to heal from that change and see the world new, maybe even brighter than before. I wasn't there yet… the world wasn't brighter, just different. At least the media exposure had died down; paps were chasing whoever was involved in the latest scandal, and I could finally come back to work.

The front door chimed. *Damn*, I thought, *I mustn't have locked the door.* We'd just closed for the day. I peeped from behind the computer screen to greet the customer. And there he was standing with two coffees in hand, small bite sized shortbread on top, his long blonde hair tied back in a ponytail.

'Hello stranger.' Levi stood there staring at me with the usual look I received from people who hadn't seen me for a while. They weren't sure what to say, but you could tell they had a hundred questions.

'Hey,' I said softly. I hadn't seen him since the dinner I'd stormed out of crying.

'I… I know I have no right to be in here, I just…' He turned towards the door.

'No, stay. Take a seat, we're closed anyway.' I walked towards the door, locking it. It was probably about time we spoke. No doubt I would still have to see him in this town, and I couldn't deal with anymore awkward energy around me.

'Did you bring me coffee?' I asked as he stood stiff, not moving an inch since the moment he walked in.

'Yeah, I did.' He passed me a cup, I bit into the shortbread sitting on the top of the lid and pointed to the lounge chairs to take a seat. 'I've walked past here with coffee so many times, but this is the first time I caught you.'

I sat down. 'This is only my second day back at work.'

'Ah… yeah, that makes sense.' We both took a sip of our coffees at the same time. 'Hey, there's lots of things that I need to say but the first one is, I'm sorry. I really am. How I acted wasn't right, I should have spoken up earlier about how I was feeling, I shouldn't have assumed we were on the same page... I....'

'It's fine Levi.' I interrupted him. 'I mean, at the time it wasn't, and I appreciate your apology. I guess well, I guess a lot has changed for me since then.'

'Yeah. It wasn't right though. I'm sorry. Can we be friends?' he asked.

'Is it okay if I say I don't know yet?' I said, crossing my arms in front of my chest.

'Yeah, I understand that.'

'I mean, coffee, catch up in the streets sure, but I don't know if we could go back to being really great mates.'

'I completely understand that.'

'I'm okay though, I just, I don't know. Like I said a lot has changed for me.'

'Yeah, I bet. If you don't mind me asking.' He squinted into my eyes, it was the same look just about everyone else in this town had been giving me over the past couple of weeks. They wanted to know the real story, the one beyond the Daily Mail. Everyone wanted my 60 Minutes Special and they wanted to be the first ones to know, but everyone seemed too shy to ask. They wanted to know how on earth we ended up on the red carpet with The Koras more than if I had any long-term brain injuries. 'What happened? I came here the following Monday with coffees to apologise about that night, I was a dick Daph, I really was, but Lisa told me you had taken a trip with the girls. The next thing, well the next thing I saw was the news...'

'I haven't told anyone what really happened. And even if I did tell you the truth, you wouldn't believe me.'

'Daph, as much as I've been a dick, you know me, try me.'

He was right, I did know him. And although he was an absolute asshole to me, I trusted him. 'It was the seminar, Tuned In, it all started after the night, well the night we last spoke. Things started to change that very next morning.'

'What do you mean?' His eyes narrowed in on me as he took another sip from his coffee cup.

'After Tuned In. Well, I got the power of manifestation. Everything I thought, everything I said, started to happen. It started with free clothes, food, drinks and next thing you know we were touring with The Koras. After the incident, the power left.'

His eyebrows didn't raise, and his mouth didn't twitch in doubt. 'Daphne, you do know that's not what the seminar is about?'

'Yes, I can't say that I went there expecting that to happen.'

Levi laughed. 'No Daph, you don't get it. I didn't recommend that seminar because of the idea of manifestation. I mentioned it because it's a wakeup call. Well, I guess, that's what it was for me. It was a wakeup call for me to stop being a leaf in the wind in my life and that if I really wanted something, I shouldn't sit and wait for it to come to me, I have the power to go and make it happen. You still have your power Daph, we all do, every single day we get out of bed.'

'That's why you started talking about what I'm going to do with my career that night. And I was too focused on the idea of a relationship?' I said, nodding slowly as I added another piece to the jumbled puzzle of events in my head.

'Your so called 'career' doesn't matter Daph. It doesn't matter at all. I know you've never said anything, but I see it in you. The spark, the things that light you up when you see a new piece of clothing or when you get to dress something. That look is rare, it's the same look I see in the surfers that come into my store. I just think you shouldn't waste that thing inside of you... I can tell that there's more in there that wants to come out... I just... when I see that look... I just don't think that anyone should rob the world of that.'

I smiled as my mind flashed back to the conversation with Kas not so long ago. His voice echoed through my mind. *I can see the light in your eyes when you talk about fashion. That look, is my favourite look in anyone.*

'I know it didn't end the way it you'd planned but there's still some amazing reviews about the style on the Aria's red carpet when you sift through the drama,' said Levi.

'I don't even want to look. I've banned myself from any media for a while… I still haven't even watched the video.' I sighed, sinking deeper into the seat and taking a sip of coffee.

'That's probably a good thing.'

I felt my phone vibrating in the pocket of my black jeans. I pulled it, looking down at the screen and once again seeing his name.

'Who's that?' Levi asked as I placed the phone down on the chair's arm rest and let it ring out.

'Just someone who calls me occasionally,' I said bluntly.

'It's him isn't it, the man kissing you in the pictures. Kas, that's his name, right? Do you still talk?'

'I said he rings. I didn't say I answered the phone calls, not that it's any of your business anyway,' I said bluntly, waiting for the phone to stop ringing.

There was a long pause as my phone finally stopped ringing. 'Sorry, you're right. I… I also heard that the other guy, he got three years.'

I nodded, pursing my lips, staring out onto the street.

'I'm sorry Daph, I really am. It's horrible, he should have got way longer than three years.'

'Three years is fine. I'm protected, I'm safe and so is Amy. And I really appreciate you coming to chat to me and bringing me coffee. I just don't think you're the person I should be talking to.'

'I know, that's fair. I should probably go anyway, there's guys waiting for me down at the beach.' He stood up out of his seat,

I followed him and held my arms out to embrace him in a hug, before sitting back down as he let himself out.

'Don't let what happened take that light in your eyes Daph.' I ignored Levi's comment as he closed the door behind him.

I took the last sip from my coffee as I sunk deeper into the chair. Staring at the racks of clothes that surrounded me. I'd missed out on the new season buying period, there were some pieces on the racks that I wouldn't have chosen. But I kept my mouth shut, Lisa had done an amazing job of keeping the store running for so long. I stared directly at one lime green crop that hung singularly by itself and I couldn't help but laugh. I sat, still laughing so loud it bought me to tears. If anyone walked past the closed glass door right now, they would have thought I may have been having some sort of emotional breakdown. I laughed at the way my whole body cringed when I walked back into work for the first time and saw the hideous crop. I laughed at Levi's unchangeable face as I told him I had a power. I laughed thinking about the first night we spent with The Koras and I fell asleep backstage on the couch. I laughed thinking that months ago, the biggest thing I wanted to manifest in my life was Levi. I laughed that in the past couple of months I'd experience more that I'd ever done in my whole life. I've never been presented with so many different emotions to deal with at once.

My memories were full of pain, loss, hurt, love, anger and fun. A lot of it still hurt, a lot of it will still hurt for a while, I was aware of that. I sighed, still staring at the green top and my laugh turned into a smile. There were some moments I would've taken back, some things that I wished had never happened. But sitting in this chair right now, I felt the most indifferent. It felt like a newness, a moment of fresh air. A chance to see the world, in a completely different shade than I ever had before, even though I was staring into lime green cotton. My eyes were fully alight.

I stood up out of the chair, picked up my phone and dialed

his number. I was nervous, pacing up and down the store. He had emailed me his Australian number weeks before, but I never called, worried he wanted to chat about bad press.

'Daphne! Darling, how are you? You wouldn't believe it but I'm standing in my Sydney store. How have you been? I'm so sorry I haven't checked in. I did get to send you flowers? Did you get them?' He spoke so quickly.

'I didn't get the flowers, I'm sorry. I didn't receive a lot of gifts that people said they had sent me though. I transferred from Sydney hospital to Ballina without anyone finding out very quickly.'

'Oh, that's lovely that you were able to get home. It is so terribly disgusting what happened to you. Usher was just telling me that man got put away for three years… it would have been for longer if the same thing happened in Italy.'

'He did. Hey, I… I'm sorry for any bad press that the incident may have caused you.'

'Bad press? Don't you worry about bad press. This is about your well-being Daphne. Besides, there is nothing wrong with a little bad press. To be honest the styling reviews were wonderful, Lana's little red number is being created by fast fashion brands everywhere now. Cheap fakes, but that doesn't matter, the whole of Australia now knows my name, which is the best news yet. But are you well? You sound well.'

'Yeah, I am,' I said, smiling widely, staring out into the middle of the empty store 'I'm really well Noah.'

'Daphne, that's so good to hear! Oh, and I must tell you I'm having lunch with Sophia Meyers tomorrow. I'm overly excited for that, she wants to do a collab.'

'A collab? With Sophia?' I was so shocked. I hadn't heard from Sophia, as far I was concerned, she hated me, she never wanted to see me again.

'Yes, she said she loved how our designs went together and she wants to create a new season limited edition collection which showcases something classic and sophisticated with a little bit of Noah edge.'

'Wow. That's great. That's not what I was expecting, but that's amazing.'

'Yes. Well, she wants to branch out to Milan and the rest of Europe, and I want to be able to do the same here in Australia, so I think creating something together is really going to help us do that,' he said. I caught a glimpse of my own smile take over my face from the full-length mirror in the corner of the store.

'I'm glad. I'm stoked by how all this has turned out, truly.'

'Yes, well I wish it had a happier ending for you…' His voice drifted off.

'Noah. This is not my ending. This is the beginning.' I stopped pacing up and down the shop and stood up tall. 'The real reason I'm calling is because I have an idea… something I have been working on for a while now, whether that's been consciously or unconsciously I'm still unsure, but I'd love your help.'

'Of course, anything. You gave me the incredible break down here I needed. How can I help you?'

'Well…'

Chapter 22

12 weeks later

'Daphne, it is so hard to catch up with you these days, what have you been up to?' Amy ran up and embraced me, before we sat down at our usual booth at the Balcony. It was true, I hadn't seen the girls in at least six weeks.

'You look and smell divine as always.' Amy smelt like one of my favourite perfumes. 'Roberto Cavalli?'

'How did you know?' Amy was wearing a slimline white linen dress with gorgeous gold hoops and matching wedges.

'It used to be my fave,' I said.

Lana walked over wearing a silky black midi dress and a clear pair of heels, carrying a tray of three margaritas. 'Sorry ladies but these ones weren't free.' Amy laughed and I rolled my eyes, grabbing one of the drinks from the tray.

'Sorry, I couldn't resist."

'I know, it's okay, I'm sure it will provide us with content to laugh about for years to come.'

'At least we can see the funny side,' said Lana.

'Not everything is to be laughed about though. In all seriousness though, how have you been doing? You've been quiet,' Amy asked.

'Some days are like magic and then some days I don't want to leave the house in case someone will take another photo of me, or recognize me from well, you know. But isn't that just life in general? Somedays are great, somedays a really shitty. I can say I do feel a lot older after this experience.' The girls nodded and took another sip.

'I know that feeling,' said Lana.

'Overall, I'm good though, I'm good. I've been working hard, and things are coming together.'

'Is it rude if I ask if you've heard from Kas?' Amy asked.

'I think the calls have finally stopped,' I said. The last phone call of his I'd let ring out was a couple of weeks ago.

'So, you haven't heard the latest news then?' she prodded.

'If I am completely honest, I've still been keeping away from any news or social media. Why's that?'

'Oh, it doesn't matter.'

'No, tell me.'

'He has announced his solo career.'

'Oh.'

'Yeah, I think it's great. I read an article online the other day how he's switching up his style. The Rolling Stone interviewed him, naming the article, The Folk Rockstar.'

'That's good,' I said bluntly, taking another large sip of my margarita. I was happy for him, I was. I knew he would make an incredible acoustic artist and that he had the freedom to create what he really wanted to go alone.

'This isn't about that tonight anyway; this is to you Amy!' Lana raised her glass, and I followed her lead.

'To Amy!' I said. I'd never seen Amy smile brighter as we clinked our glasses together.

'I'm really going to miss you guys so much though!' she said.

'You won't miss us, because we are going to be travelling up as much as possible, this gives us a chance to head to Melbourne and enjoy free accommodation whenever we want too,' I said.

'Yeah, what is your living situation down there? Have you found a place yet?' said Lana.

'Not yet, I have been searching on Flatmates and I have a couple of places and people I've organised to meet with next Sunday, but they have put me up in a hotel for three weeks so I'm not in a huge rush.'

'Wow, they must be really stoked to have you on board!' I said.

'Well, let's be honest, could you blame them? I was born for this role! Born for it! And finally, someone has seen this,' Amy called out in her most dramatic acting voice. We all laughed.

'So, Daphne, are you going to turn back on the media now that Amy is the voice for pop culture?' said Lana.

'Only to your channel, of course.'

'Catch me every Saturday from 10 a.m. to 12 p.m. on E!'

'What's the show going to be called?' I asked.

'It's essentially an Australian spin off of Entertainment Tonight. It's Entertainment Aus. E! have given us the nod to go ahead with ten episodes and judge ratings from there. So, who knows girls I could be back in a couple of months? I hope I'm not. Because I was specifically told I'm not allowed to step foot back into my old office again,' Amy rolled her eyes and I laughed.

I couldn't stop smiling for Amy, how she had managed to turn the crazy press around to becoming the Anchorwoman of a brand-new show on one of the biggest networks astounded me, she was unstoppable that woman. It inspired me.

'Don't be stupid, you won't be back in a couple of months. I would almost put money on it you'll be calling us letting us know you're off to LA for an even bigger opportunity,' I said.

'Oh Daph, if only you still had your powers.' Amy sighed.

'Seriously though, we're so freaking happy for you. And you have to give us regular updates, I need to know everything about what it's like to be on T.V., all the incredible people that you get to meet, what it's like to live in Melbourne… Where to get the best margs… everything,' Lana said to Amy.

'Duh, you guys are going to be on my speed dial for absolutely everything that happens to me thousands of kilometers away.'

'I'm glad,' I said.

'Oh my gosh, Lana how was last night?' Amy almost jumped out of her seat like she had forgotten an extremely important appointment.

'What happened last night?' I asked.

'It was date number three,' said Lana.

'Date number three? With who? How did I miss out on one and two?' I looked at her shocked.

'Like we said Daph, you've been quiet,' Amy butted in. They were right, I couldn't disagree. It wasn't just Kas's calls I hadn't been picking up lately, it was most peoples'.

'I'm sorry, so who's the lucky guy?'

'Corey. He's a young surgeon who just transferred to the Ballina hospital. We locked eyes in surgery for a knee replacement.' Lana handed me her phone, with his Instagram profile open. The pictures showed a 30ish-old-looking man with light brown curly hair. He was fit, tall, attractive, with the warmest smile.

'Wait, is he an iron man?' I clicked on one of the photos, gaining a closer look of a tall shredded man in speedos running out of the water with the caption—*another race down*.

'Yeah, he competes on weekends.' Lana's dimples gleamed as I handed her phone back.

'So, date one?'

'We had a couple more surgeries together, and some small talk after each procedure before he asked me out. But finally, two weeks ago, he asked me if I wanted to join him at the new restaurant opening of Kansas.'

'Stop, you've been? How was it?' I asked.

'Amazing, can't recommend highly enough, you should really check it out. Anyway, we had an amazing dinner, and finished the night with a beach walk and a kiss.'

'And date two?'

'I'm getting to it.' I loved seeing the smile on Lana's face and hearing her get excited over someone new. Jack had fallen off the face of the earth after we came back home. No one had heard from him. Although, getting an explanation probably didn't help with the fact I still wasn't picking up Kas's calls. For a moment I paused, looking at Lana stare at the photos of her new crush. Maybe she'd heard from Jack. Maybe she'd spoken to Kas. I knew he had her number. With the amount of times he'd called me, surely he'd tried to get in contact with her. I knew the girls were being protective of me, they didn't speak too much about the situation and I pretended that my heart still didn't miss him. I shook my head, trying not to let my mind dive deep into made-up stories.

'Date two was on Wednesday, we went bowling and grabbed Ramen. And then last night he took me to see Terry Owens, the comedian. Which I also highly recommend. I spent the whole night trying not to wet my pants. He really is the sweetest guys, he is so lovely and generous and caring and sweet and fit and attractive and intelligent,' Lana swooned.

'So, when do we get to meet him?' Amy cut off Lana before she could get too carried away with her endless list of attributes.

'I don't know Little Miss "I'm moving to Melbourne in a couple of days",' said Lana. 'Daphne you'll have to meet us for a drink sometime, maybe just give it a couple more weeks first.'

'Don't worry Amy, I'll give you the honest feedback on the Iron Man Surgeon.' I laughed. 'I'm happy for you Lana, he sounds lovely.'

'Perfect,' Amy said, taking the last sip of her margarita, then standing up in the booth, shaking her empty glass towards the bar. Then pointed three fingers up in the air.

'Amy!' Lana scowled as she sat back down.

'What? Jake's working the bar tonight, he'll bring us over three.'

'So, Daphne, when do we get to find out about all this secret stuff you've been working on and too busy to catch up with us for?' Lana stared at me wide-eyed.

'Yeah Daph, it's about time you spilled the beans,' Amy said, mimicking Lana's stare.

'Soon, I promise, and you both know that you'll be the very first people to know. So, when are you seeing Corey again?' I quickly changed the conversation.

Amy and Lana rolled their eyes. 'Fine keep your secrets. He's taking me for brunch tomorrow morning, and then we're going to head out for a hike, weather permitting.'

'Oh, the dates are becoming a lot more regular. Wait have you slept with him yet?'

'No, I haven't. And I know it sounds weird, but I'm nervous to. It will happen when it happens. I guess I just really like this guy. He really is different than the rest.'

'Here's hoping.' Amy cynically raised her glass.

'Don't worry, I still believe in your judgement Lana.' I smiled back at her.

Jake walked over with a tray of fresh margs, placing them down on the table and replacing the tray with our empty glasses. 'These ones are on the house ladies.'

'Why's that?' I asked, feeling a little more cautious around accepting free drinks.

'I hear we're losing one of our most regular customers tonight.'

'Oh Jake, that's so lovely. Don't worry, you won't miss me too much. I'll be back in for a marg every time I'm home, you can count on that.' Amy smiled.

'You better. Never forget where the best tequila is when you're in the big smoke.'

'You'll always be my number one bartender Jake.' Amy blew him a kiss as he walked away.

'Well, the first round was for me, I say this round is for us.

It's been a wild six months, but there's no one else I would have wanted go through any of this with.'

'Right back at you girl,' I said clinking our glasses together.

'I'm excited for what's to come,' Lana said.

'Same, but I feel like this is the end of an era Amz, this has been our spot since we could legally drink. It's going to be really different without you here.' I pouted my lips at her.

'I know, but hey it's not just me that's changing and moving on.' She stared through me as she took a sip. 'I think this has been coming for all of us for a long time. It's just finally all happening at once.'

'When it rains it pours,' said Lana.

'I can't wait to see where we all end up in a year. I hope we magically end up back here drinking margs, exchanging stories on all our adventures.'

Chapter 23

12 months later

'It's perfect, you don't have to play with them anymore.' I leaned over to Lisa, patting her on the back as she fidgeted with the bouquets of flowers that sat on each small table.

'The aesthetics are amazing Daph, Lisa you've done an incredible job.' Amy threw her arms around me from behind, hugging my waist. 'I can't believe it's the day!'

'Thank you for being here, it means a lot.'

'Are you kidding me, I wouldn't miss this for the world,' said Amy, releasing her embrace.

I took a deep breath and looked up at the clock behind me. 'There's a line outside Daph, are you ready to let them in?' Noah said, approaching me with a glass of champagne.

'Let's just give it two minutes,' I said, taking a sip of the champagne. I walked over towards the glass front of Duskk that we had blacked out for the event. 'Eeek. It sounds like there are so many people out there.'

'I told you Daph, it's a sold-out event,' said Noah.

'Noah, thank you, I wouldn't have been able to do any of this without your help. You've been so amazing.'

'Hey, stop it. Thank yourself, you've worked your little butt off to get here darling, this whole thing is yours, it's your night. It's your time to shine.'

'It's not my night, it's our night.' I pointed to everyone in the room, Noah, Lisa, Amy and Lana. 'And it's their night,' I said, pointing to the noise outside. 'It's not my baby anymore, it's time to share it with the world.'

'And on that note, I think I should open the doors,' said Lisa.

◆ ◆ ◆

'Girl, it's only been an hour and Lisa hasn't stopped at the till, maybe we should have made more,' Noah whispered to me as the night was in full force. Duskk was filled with young women and men, trying on all the pieces, drinking wine, enjoying food. I hadn't seen anyone walk out yet. People were still coming in and every third person was holding a shopping bag.

'I know, it's crazy. I'm going to need to contact our suppliers first thing tomorrow.' Amy approached me, weaving through the crowd holding a cordless microphone. 'Okay, I'm going to start my speech. Do you think?' I felt a hand on tap on my back and I spun around.

My mouth dropped open in shock. She stood staring at me, her long brown hair tied back in a low ponytail. 'Jesse?' I said, I still remembered her name after all this time.

'Yes, I thought I recognised you. Daphne right? And this is your show?'

'Yes,' I said slowly nodding. 'Hey um, can we chat?' I turned back to Noah and Amy. 'Just give me one minute.' Before Jesse could answer I grabbed hold of her arm and weaved through the crowd cornering her near the changerooms.

'What are you doing here?' I said.

She laughed. 'Whoa, calm down. I'm just on a weekend vacation and I saw that this opening was on so I thought I would pop in. Is that okay? Or would you like me to leave?'

I took a deep breath and a step back so that I wasn't too close to her face. 'No it's fine. Thank you for coming.' I sighed.

'Is your boyfriend here?' she asked. I furrowed my brow, until memories flooded back of our first conversation.

'Oh, no,' I said.

Jesse smiled. 'Okay, I'm not being that honest. I did see the papers a while back and when I saw your name on the shop outside, I was curious. It happened to you, didn't it? You were the girl of last year, the one that got the power.'

My eyes widened and I gulped down. I leaned in closer to her, speaking just loud enough so she could hear me over the music, but not so loud that anyone could listen in. 'You know about it?'

Jessie laughed and nodded. 'Yeah, I've been one of Casey's little projects before. She picks someone from the crowd who she knows doesn't really get it and well, you know what happens next,' she said.

'But I had it, and then it was gone. No one told me how I got it or how it left, but it's definitely not here anymore,' I said.

'And isn't that wonderful? You've created this yourself. Not from a stupid power,' she said, looking around the room.

'Yes, but please tell me what it was,' I said, my eyes glued on hers.

'To be honest, I don't know either. I never got an answer from Casey. She brushes it off or ignores everyone that it happens to as though it doesn't even exist. I guess the magician can never give away the secret to their real magic tricks,' she said. 'And by looking at what you've created here. I don't think you need to question it anymore, I can see you're on your path.'

'But you must know something, anything. Jesse please you have to give me some answers,' I said. Crossing my arms in front of my chest I stood taller.

Jesse laughed. 'Look, I hardly know you. But if there's anything I've learnt from the people who have said to catch the power from a Tuned In seminar, including myself, it's that they're going there and they're heading down the wrong path. It's a complete theory. But I believe having the power speeds it up, drops you deep so that you have to find your own way out and in doing so, redirects you to where you're really meant to be. The power gives you nothing but the very gift of rock bottom, and like I said, it's very obvious it's done its job for you.' Jesse smiled, winked and shrugged all at the same time.

Amy walked in between us, grabbing hold of my arm. Just as I did Jesse's before. 'I'm sorry to interrupt. But I've got to take the star of the night with me now,' said Amy.

'It's okay, I've got to go now too,' said Jesse. Amy flashed her a polite smile and then pulled me back through the crowd. I kept my eyes on Jessie as she weaved her way back towards the front door.

Amy flicked the switch on the microphone, stood up tall and said, 'Welcome, ladies and gentlemen. Welcome to a fine night at Duskk. Thank you for coming out to the official launch of Australia's hottest new label, Ms. You.' Everyone took a step back, as Amy started talking, including Noah, creating a circle around Amy and me.

'I'm Amy Atherton and I will be your host for this evening. As we go through the night, I'll be chatting to you about the different pieces of Ms. You's first collection and how they came to be. The best ways to style them as well as giving you sneak peaks of what to expect in the future.' Amy paused, dazzling the room with her best on-stage smile. 'Instead of a catwalk tonight, we've done something a little bit different. You'll find certain people, that I will embarrassingly point our right now, wearing our favourite Ms. You pieces. You can see how each of us have styled it differently, how they look on different bodies. Myself, Lana, where are you Lana? Give the crowd a wave.' Lana who was deep in the crowd to our left, gave a small wave and did a spin in the lilac blazer dress. 'And Lisa.' Lisa waved from her spot behind the counter. She was wearing the crisp white wide-leg pant paired with the white lace corset. 'And of course, if you do want to try anything on yourself tonight, you're more than welcome to use the changerooms down the back. And of course, Daphne...' Amy held her arm out towards me and I did a shy curtsey. I was wearing the full-length black silk split dress matched with snakeskin boots, paired with my favourite red lip. Amy threw me a smile and grabbed my hand. 'The founder of Ms. You, happens to be one of my very best friends, Daphne Waters. When Daphne first showed me her design and everything that Ms. You stands for, I was blown away. And it's a real honour tonight to be here, not only wearing this stunning label, but also introducing Daphne tonight so that she can tell you more about the birth of this stunning brand and the fabulous new clothes that you are now holding in your shopping bags. So, without, further adieu let me introduce the lady who made this happen— Daphne.'

Amy passed me the microphone and the room broke out into an applause. 'Thank you, thank you everyone. It truly means a lot to me that you are here celebrating the birth of my baby, Ms. You. I know it sounds strange but today does feel like a birth of some sort. I'm sure anyone who is in a creative industry can understand what it means to dedicate yourself to something, put part of you into something and then to give it to the world as a gift. It's been an incredible journey of ups and downs and frustrations to get here today, but I'm really glad I'm here and I'm glad that you're all hear celebrating with me and enjoying what Ms. You has become and what the label stands for today.'

I paused to look around at all the faces in the room. Most of them were women, some of them were men, they all stood staring at me, light smiles waiting for me to say my next words. It was a surreal feeling. As though I knew exactly who everyone was in the room, even though the majority were strangers... but they were holding my bags. So, I did know them, I knew exactly who they were. They were the women I'd created this brand for.

They were who I'd thought about every day on this journey. They were me.

'Ms. You has been a dream come true, that for most of my life I didn't even know I was dreaming, I didn't know what I was subconsciously creating. Ms. You has been birthed from all my life experiences, the good, the bad, the boring, the momentous and everything in between.' Amy placed her hand on my shoulder, and I continued. 'Ms. You is my creative representation for what it means to be a young woman in the 21st century. Ms. You is lost as fuck...' The crowd broke out into warm smiles and laughter. 'Lost and beautiful, creating a path that is not linear. Ms. You is multifaceted. She tries to stay in her lane but loves to wander. She's innocent, yet wild. Naïve but incredibly intelligent. Most of all she stays curious, she questions, she flows, she doesn't have a clear path. She changes with the seasons as she needs. She's edgy but safe, she's dark and light. She represents the polarity through life.' I paused, I caught Lana's eye in the crowd, her head nodding at me. Noah's smile widened.

'I guess that's what Ms. You is about. And what I want it to provide every single woman here tonight in their wardrobes. I want Ms. You to be able to be the brand you can turn to when you don't know what you want, when you need something to showcase a fleeting feeling, or a soul calling... when you want to try something out that is so far away from your comfort zone, or something that gives you the feeling like you've finally come home. Ms. You represents all of us, in any moment. Somewhere between mess and structure, sex and solitude, warm and cold. I really hope that you enjoy the first collection, and I can't wait to make many, many more.' I handed the microphone back to Amy and the crowd started clapping and cheering, someone at the back left whistled and my smile broke out into laughter.

'Can everyone raise a glass to my amazing friend, founder and designer of Ms. You Daphne.' Everyone raised their class in unison, and I bit my lip, hoping to hold back the tears of happiness. 'Please don't forget if you are taking pictures tonight, or in future wearing your new outfits, tag on Instagram @MsYouTheLabel. Enjoy shopping lovelies, I'll check in soon.' Amy flicked off the mic, placing it down, and the music throughout Duskk raised again.

Lana came running towards us, weaving through people so quick I don't know how she didn't tread on anyone's toes. 'My girl, I'm so freaking proud!' She embraced me in a hug. 'And I have to be completely honest with you, I don't think I have had as many compliments on an outfit till today, this is my new go-to.'

Corey walked up behind her, kissing her on the back of the head. 'Yeah, you've really created something special here Daph, I think you've found your thing.'

'I think so too,' I replied confidently.

'I'm proud of you Daph,' said James, wrapping his arms around me. 'I've got to go, but I'll see you at home later yeah?'

I nodded. 'You will, thanks for coming.'

'So, when can I get my hands on the next collection, I have to wear this on air before it's even launched,' said Amy.

'Oh, don't worry, you're in my marketing plan.' I winked.

'Good, I better be,' said Amy. I laughed and leaned in, giving her a hug.

I felt a tap on my back and as I swung around...

My jaw dropped open and my body froze. There he was, standing tall. His eyes were clear, staring deep into mine. He didn't smile, in fact, he looked nervous. I could see his words spinning in his head before he spoke.

'Hey Daph...' he finally said. I didn't move.

'I called Kas about tonight.' Lana took a step forward, intersecting our energy. I didn't look at her, I kept my eyes right on Kas. I wasn't shocked, I'd thought long ago that they were still talking.

'If you want me to leave, I completely understand, it's not my place to be here. I just, I just really wanted to congratulate you.'

I turned towards Lana, Corey and Amy. 'I'm just going to step outside for a second.'

Lana nodded, taking a step back and Kas followed my lead as I snuck out the front door.

'I called. I called many times,' he said as he closed the door behind him.

'I know you did.' I swung around to face him. 'I didn't answer because I didn't want to speak to you. It's been over a year Kas, I don't want this bought up again, not on my night.'

'I wanted to see you. I haven't gone a day without thinking about you. And look at you, look what you've created. I... I'm in awe. I couldn't stay away anymore. I just had to see you.' He reached out to touch my hand but I pulled away. 'All this time, I've been asking Lana for updates. I'm sorry please don't hate her. I hounded her at the start. I needed to know that you where okay..'

I stood speechless, staring at him.

'I understand how you might feel around me, I understand it brings up the past, I understand you don't feel safe, and now I've come here on your launch night. I'm so sorry.'

I opened my mouth but no words came out.

'I'm sorry Daph, I should have protected you, this should have never happened,' he said, his eyes locked on mine full of sorrow, his hand reached out to mine but he quickly pulled it away as I held mine behind my back.

'It's no one's fault, no one could have predicted what happened. I'm not excusing his behavior, and yes, I believe he should have been given a longer sentence some days. But what happened, happened and we can't take it back. I'm okay, and I won't let it define me. You can release the guilt now,' I said.

'This isn't how I wanted this to go,' he said, his voice croaky.

'We haven't spoken about anything. I haven't seen you since that night, I know that's because I've avoided you but, how did you expect it would go?' I snapped.

'Honestly, I don't know. I knew you probably didn't want to see me. I was going to hide in the background, I just wanted to see you, see you shine, see that light in your eyes again,' he said. I looked away from his gaze, blinking quickly trying to hold back tears. His voice felt so sincere.

I sighed. 'Let's sit,' I said, gesturing to the sidewalk.

'Are you sure? There's a whole party going on in there without you.' He pointed back to the front door.

'It's not my party anymore, I've done my work, it's Ms. You's. She's in there shining on her own,' I said, taking a seat. Kas sat down next to me on the edge of the sidewalk, our legs dangling out onto the quiet street.

I sighed out, relaxing my shoulders, staring out into the dark stores on the other side of the street, dimly lit up by the streetlights. Even though I'd tried my best to block out any thoughts of Kas, there were moments where I wondered if I would ever be in the exact position I currently was. If there would ever be a chance, I happened to run into him and I could ask him everything I wanted to. Tell him everything I needed to. I had the perfect spiel mapped out in my head, but sitting here next to him, my mind felt empty.

'It's all just a blur…' I finally said. 'The whole thing, the whole time with you. It's just a blur.'

'I can understand that,' he said, biting his lip.

'It's not just the trauma of the situation. It's everything. It provided me the most horrific moment of my life, that lived on for months. I was in hiding, trying to recover for months until the media calmed down. I guess that's why I avoided your calls. I wanted to forget everything, I wanted to pretend it never happened.'

'I can understand that too.' He spoke so calm, listening to my every word.

'But it was never you that hurt me, I'd just associated you with the situation.'

He didn't speak, he just stared at me, his eyes gleamed with sorrow and love. I could tell he wanted to reach out, to touch me, but he was nervous. I turned towards him, catching his eye.

'It's so weird, it's been so long, so much time has passed. We're probably completely different people now.' I paused, looking into the lines in his eyes I could still see so intricately even in the night light. 'I don't feel like this has ended, I never spoke to you, I never resolved it.'

'Hey, you had every right not to answer my calls. I understand, trust me I do. I know what you mean, the feeling of something still being left open, unresolved. I guess that's part of why I felt so drawn to you, how much I needed to see you, hear about you, make sure that you were okay.'

I gulped down and took a deep breath, still in shock that he was here. I know he cared; I know he always did. But my mind was running wild, thinking about all the reasons as to why he came back. After all this time, after how much I'd ignored him, blocked him out of my life. But none of the stories mattered. 'I promised myself if I ever saw you again, I would ask you three questions.'

'You can ask me anything you want Daph.'

'What happened after that night? I... I'm ready to know the complete truth.'

He took a deep breath. 'The actual incident was a complete blur to me too. I didn't see him hit you but I saw you fall and well I guess you've seen the rest.'

'I haven't. I didn't watch it. I'll never watch it. I don't want to.'

'Oh, I didn't know. I saw you fall in motion.' His bottom lip started to shake as he slowly pieced together his words. 'I tried to catch you, but it was too late. You were out cold, lying there on the ground, looking so small. Everyone came running, and I was pushed away so quick. I went to run to you, to follow you out on the stretcher, come to the hospital with you, but we were all handcuffed and taken into custody by the police. I thought you were dead Daph. It was horrible. I… I realised how lucky I was to have met someone so…' He paused, gulping down. 'When we were all getting questioned, I saw red. I launched at Eli at the same time as everyone else. He was locked up and after the questioning we were sent free. I called Lana and well, that was the last time I heard from you.'

'But after that, this whole year, what you've gone through, the whole situation. I want to know it all.'

'Daph, I haven't had to deal with half the hardship that you have had to move through after that, this isn't about me at all.'

'No, I just want to know. I want to know everything.'

'After our conversation, I knew you didn't want to see me, I knew you'd headed home to recover so I thought I would give you your space. But it was so hard Daph. I couldn't help but call. Like you said, maybe I just needed closure, maybe I just needed to know you were okay. But then seeing you again tonight. I… I'm proud of you Daph, you've done it all, everything you wanted, this is incredible,' he said, pointing back at the party inside.

I looked away, staring down at the street. Together we sat in silence, listening the muffled sound of chatter and music coming from Duskk.

'I listened to your EP,' I said, finally breaking the silence, looking back up at him. 'I think you're doing the same.' Kas smiled, not taking his eyes off me. I'd never forgotten his glowing green eyes; they were a stained memory still clearly visible when I closed mine.

'After Eli got sentenced, we all decided to go our separate ways. We cancelled the American tour, Matty was already playing for another band, so he joined them full time and Jack just wanted to take off and travel alone. If I'm honest, I've hardly heard from him. I guess that pushed me into going it alone, starting my solo career. It's been good, I like it, it's different but I think I was ready. It's what I needed and getting away from the boys has been a blessing in disguise, I think we could all say that.'

'I'm happy for you,' I said with no emotion. I was, I was happy. I'd smiled when I first heard his music, but I felt as though a cage was around my heart. It wanted to jump out and hug him, but it was locked away, rattling the edges.

'That was question one, what's question number two?' Kas grinned sheepishly.

'Tell me why you really came here,' I said. Holding back my tears came out in anger, but it didn't stop them flowing. 'Why did you really want to see me? Was it just to see that I was okay? Is this really just for closure?'

'No.' He paused and took a deep breath. 'You're the most impactful person I've ever met in my life Daphne. In so many ways, and you don't even know it.' This time, I couldn't hold it back any longer. I bit the inside of my lip and a single tear fell down my cheek. Kas wiped it away and held his hand on the side of my face. My mind flashed back to the last time he did that. The first time we kissed, sitting on the edge of the hotel room bed in Sydney.

'You're awe-inspiring to me Daphne, from the very first moment I met you. Your whole presence exudes this. You're a go-getter, a big believer, dreamer. Sometimes you hide behind shyness or self-doubt and insecurity, but it doesn't stop you. Everything you said in there, about Ms. You, it's you. And you've not only gifted yourself this amazing business and creative passion, you've empowered the hell out of every woman in there tonight, to show up exactly as they are as well. I'd be lying if you didn't do the same for me.' I turned towards the door as I heard a group of girls leave Duskk. They seemed a little tipsy, talking loudly, walking up the street, they didn't notice us.

'I love it.'

'I love our new clothes.'

'Ms. You is my go-to, how amazing that this is available in our tiny town!'

'See,' Kas said, sliding in closer to me, hiding my face from the door as more people started to leave. Tears flowed but they were tears of gratitude as I broke into a smile.

'I know it sounds stupid… especially after all this time. But I love you Daph.' His voice strained and his green eyes wept.

My breath caught in my throat, and I felt a warmth tingle along the insides of my chest, growing bigger with every moment. 'So, we were we real? That was actually going to be my third question,' I said. I returned the favour, wiping the tears from his cheeks as he smiled.

'I hoped we were real. I mean I hope this is real. It feels like the realest thing I've ever experienced. All this time later and I… I can't let you go. It kills me to know that I was involved in one of the most horrific moments of your life. You deserve the best Daph. I know we can't erase the past and we shouldn't. But I want to start over.'

I didn't speak. My heart felt as though it was about to burst throughout my whole body, but not with pain. With happiness, with light, with love.

'Can I ask you something…' he said.

'Sure.'

'Did you feel the same?'

'Did or do…'

'Do you feel the same?'

'This whole time. This whole time I've been trying to hide it. But I haven't been able to stop thinking about you.'

His eyes widened as the words escaped from my mouth and

he moved in closer, gently placing his lips on mine, just like the first time.

Our lips parted but our eyes stayed still.

'I can't believe I was lucky enough to meet you,' he said.

'It still baffles me too…' If only he knew how much.

'C'mon,' said Kas, taking my hand. 'We're missing out on your very own party.' He pulled me up off the street, and I snuggled into his chest as he held me tight. My whole body relaxing into his arms. He kissed my forehead.

'What does this mean?' I whispered.

'It means I'd like to spend more time here, with you. If that's okay with you?' he said.

I nodded, smiling. 'I'd like that a lot,' I said.

'Would I be pushing it, if, maybe, I asked if you would like to be my girlfriend?' he said, his voice softened and his cheeks turned pink. I grabbed hold of both his hands. I couldn't wipe the grin of my face.

'Honestly, that sounds perfect, boyfriend,' I said with a wink. It did, it felt relaxed and so right. Kas squeezed me tight again, this time meeting my lips. I'd missed the taste of his, I could have stayed locked in his hold and his kiss for longer, but he pulled away whispering in my ear.

'We've got forever for this, but right now, I can't let you miss out on your party.' Kas led me back through the front door.

◆ ◆ ◆

The crowd had dwindled, but each person leaving had their arms filled with shopping bags. 'We've almost sold out. You're right. We should have made more. We'll need to order twice as much, first thing in the morning,' said Noah, 'This isn't like me, I've never gotten the ordering wrong before,' he said a little frazzled.

I grinned, looking around at the empty hangers. 'It's okay

Noah, we'll get more stock ASAP.'

'Hey Daph, there you are.' Amy lightly tapped me on the back. 'We're going to head to the Balcony,' she pointed towards Lana and Corey standing next to her, 'do you both want to come?' I looked back, Lisa was standing at the doorway.

'You guys go and have fun. I'll lock up and we can clean up in the morning.'

'Thanks Lisa.' I smiled back at her. I had been so deep in conversation I hadn't heard the party start to leave.

'We'd love to,' Kas replied before I had a chance. I gazed at him, smiling. Out of the corner of my eye I could see Lana and Amy smirking at each other, seeing Kas and I so clearly wrapped up in each other.

He held out his hand. 'Are you ready? he asked, standing up.

I bit my lip and then smiled, intertwining my fingers into his. 'I'm ready.'

Shawline Publishing Group Pty Ltd
www.shawlinepublishing.com.au

SHAWLINE
PUBLISHING
GROUP

CPSIA information can be obtained
at www.ICGtesting.com
Printed in the USA
LVHW012054101022
730380LV00013B/582

9 781922 850539